UNDERSTRIKE

'Here, let me help you with that.' Seidler pulled up on his side of the box, disclosing a first layer of tissue paper.

Boysie and Siedler must have both realised the dreadful mistake at the same moment – just as the lid came free. Joe Seidler's hand was outstretched over the tissue. He stood no chance. The tissue stirred and crackled, then seemed to burst upwards like an opening flower. The long, thin body flashed out from its paper retreat and streaked with lightning speed and grace, fastening its dripping little mouth hard onto Siedler's wrist. He gave a shriek of terror. Boysie took a half step back then stopped, fascinated, screwed to the floor, hands paralysed with horror. Chicory turned and began to scream, a forearm thrown across her face as though in defence. The revolting, deadly fangs of the eight-foot black mamba had closed tightly and were relentlessly pumping venom into Siedler's bloodstream.

D0762572

Also by John Gardner in *Star*

THE LIQUIDATOR
MADRIGAL
AMBER NINE
FOUNDER MEMBER

UNDERSTRIKE

John Gardner

A STAR BOOK

published by
the Paperback Division of
W. H. ALLEN & Co. Ltd.

A Star Book
Published in 1980
by the Paperback Division of
W. H. Allen & Co. Ltd
A Howard and Wyndham Company
44 Hill Street, London W1X 8LB

First published in Great Britain by
Frederick Muller Ltd., 1965
Published by Transworld Publishers Ltd., 1966

Copyright © John Gardner, 1965

Printed in Great Britain by
Hunt Barnard Printing, Ltd., Aylesbury, Bucks.

ISBN 0 352 304588

For Orlando

This book is sold subject to the condition that it shall
not, by way of trade or otherwise, be lent,
re-sold, hired out or otherwise circulated without the
publisher's prior consent in any form of
binding or cover other than that in which it is published
and without a similar condition including this
condition being imposed on the subsequent purchaser

Double, double toil and trouble.
MACBETH : IV. I William Shakespeare

CONTENTS

INTRODUCTION 9

PROLOGUE: DOUBLE L Moscow, June 11

I. CABLE 19

II. CHICORY 39

III. ... AND LEAVE THE DRIVING TO US 58

IV. SOLEV 82

V. B+P+T=C 100

VI. UNDER... 120

VII. ... STRIKE 145

EPILOGUE: DOUBLE DATE. San Diego, July 173

INTRODUCTION TO THE
BOYSIE OAKES BOOKS

John Gardner

Someone, somewhere, has quoted me as saying – 'The Boysie
Oakes series was born out of an idea for a comic situation, a
desire to send up a particular genre at a particular time.' I have
no doubt that I said just that. It is true, but it did not start
that way.

In the early 1960s, the fantasy and fantastic world of James
Bond books ruled – okay – though the films had not quite
arrived with their injection of humour. Len Deighton's grey
poetry of espionage had only just peeped over the horizon,
and John Le Carre's first masterpiece, *The Spy Who Came In
From The Cold*, was yet to be published and acclaimed.

We were in the middle of the Cold War which was, to any
thinking person, a serious business. Yet, in popular fiction, the
swashbuckling Bond carried the day, saving the world from
villains larger than life. There were, I thought, two ways of
writing in an entertaining manner about the war of espionage.
One could play it straight, or one could be satirical. I chose
the latter and Boysie Oates was born, as it happened, on top
of a bus in Warwickshire. We were passing a clump of oak
trees when an old lady spoke sharply to her irritating grand-
child who was intent on hurling himself from one end of the
bus to the other – 'Oh come here and be a good little boysie.'
Boysie Oakes.

That night I sat down to write what I thought was going to
be a great serious satirical novel. What came out was broad
comedy well mixed with suspense.

Oakes revealed himself as a bungling, sex-orientated, immature idiot caught up against his will in a world of mayhem, death, double-dealing and secret destruction. The books have, again elsewhere, been described as 'broad, glossy black comedy.' If they are that, then I hope they are first and last entertaining black comedy. In some aspects, I am certain that they have dated, for attitudes have changed in the decade since the first – *The Liquidator* – became a bestseller. But the fantasies remain, as, I think, does the comedy, and heaven knows we need some comedy in this grey world of inflation, terrorism and dehumanisation.

Presumably, if the comedy is still there, then, in spite of change and progress, the suspense cannot be far away. I know from my mail that Oakes is still enjoyed by many people. I trust that this new edition will bring some laughs and not a few thrills.

PROLOGUE: DOUBLE L
Moscow, June

IT WAS warm. Too warm for Khavichev, who, after suffering ten minutes of the stifling heat in the long room, had opened one of the tall velvet-curtained windows. Now he leaned out, hands heavy on the sill, his closely-cropped hair showing like corn stubble to the sun. To his left Khavichev could see the whorled domes of St. Basil's Cathedral, a bright gingerbread house alone in the cobbled vastness of Red Square. Across the road, the Lenin Museum formed a rusty backdrop to the straggling sightseers jostling their way into the square to stare, or stand silent in the great queue which snaked from the Lenin Mausoleum. Below, among the foreigners with their expensive cine cameras, the sweating city men in slack formal suits, and the visiting countryfolk, drab even in floral dresses, he caught sight of a little knot of teenagers—gaudy in make-up and mock leather aping the West—the stilyagi, Moscow's jet-set. Khavichev remembered, with some misgivings, the article passed to him from Central Information last year—clipped from the London *Sunday Times*—claiming that young Russian girls were clamouring for black nylon underwear. Dangerous decadence, he thought, withdrawing his head and turning back into the room.

Khavichev was a big man, in all senses of the word. Six feet two inches in his stockinged feet, with shoulders like the back of a well-padded armchair. His face was hard—the texture of old oak bark—rarely showing emotion. His eyes were the only feature which in any way betrayed the full potential danger of the man. "Khavichev's eyes," the President of the Supreme

Soviet had once remarked, "have the power of an expertly-handled whip. They never look at you. They either flick, lash or caress."

At this moment the eyes were flicking—as they always did when something big was imminent. For, like all men who had found success in high authority, Boris Piotr Khavichev—Director of Soviet Counter-Espionage and Subversive Activities—knew his limitations. He was always a shade nervous, a trifle more wary, when planning an operation which strayed near to the breaking point of his self-known power.

He glanced at his watch. Three-ten. The meeting was scheduled, as always, for three-fifteen. He walked to the big kidney-shaped table, his slight limp—the relic of a parried knife-thrust in a Tangier alley—barely perceptible. Taking his place in the centre chair, Khavichev looked up at the oblong cinema screen which stretched blandly over the far wall. The fingers of his left hand strayed slowly down the line of little coloured buttons, set in series conveniently by the leather blotter. He pressed the button outlined in blue and spoke into the microphone desk set which connected him with the projection room high in the wall behind.

"Is everything ready?"

"All is prepared, Comrade General." The answer came pat from the loudspeaker above the screen.

"We will see the special film first. Before the main business. We will need the mosaics of San Diego later."

"Very good, Comrade General."

Khavichev pressed the white button. As though he had operated a spring mechanism, the door to the right of the screen whipped open. A young army lieutenant clicked into the room.

"Comrade General?"

"We will not be long. He has arrived?"

"He is here now, Comrade General. You wish to see him?"

"It should not be necessary. He knows what to do?"

"Exactly."

"Good. I will ring when we need him."

"Yes, Comrade."

"When we have seen him you may take him straight back to the villa. He has a lesson with Professor Engler at four, I believe."

The lieutenant nodded. Khavichev made a sharp upward gesture with the back of his outstretched hand. A signal of dismissal. The lieutenant stiffened to attention, then turned, closing the door behind him. Almost at the same moment the main double doors of the room were thrown open by the two uniformed guards—always on duty in this part of the building on Tuesday afternoons, the regular time for the weekly conference of Heads of Staff.

Khavichev rose, his lips forming the hint of a smile as he greeted his Departmental Chiefs: Archeyev of Naval Intelligence, young, slim, with that faint trace of effeminacy which often stamps naval officers who are wedded to the sea alone; Porovsky, Head of Military Counter-Espionage, stocky, with the unmistakable ruthlessness of a former OGPU man; and Varlamov, Commander of Strategic Air Espionage, a pompous, sarcastic face hiding an alert brain which carried—Khavichev often feared—more secrets than any other in Russia.

One of the soldiers quickly circled the windows, softly pulling the drapes. The two large chandeliers flashed into light.

After the usual formalities, the doors were closed and the four men took their places at the table. Khavichev unbuttoned the top of his tight jacket, cleared his throat, and began to speak: precisely, without any apparent interest in what he was saying: using the minimum number of words to convey the maximum information.

"Before we start the main business, comrades, there is a surprise I have been saving for you. We are to see a film. It concerns one man. Study him closely. He should be of particular interest to you, Comrade Varlamov." He glanced quickly towards the airforce man and touched the blue button. The lights went out and the screen became filled with coloured life.

The picture showed London's Whitehall: the camera pausing

for a moment at the Cenotaph before zooming in to focus close on a nondescript door. The door opened and a man came out into the watery sunshine, stopping at the edge of the pavement in an attempt to hail a taxi. The camera zoomed closer and Khavichev gave a satisfied smile as he heard Varlamov's slight intake of breath. The man in the picture was tall with a well-balanced athlete's body. By Western standards the face was undeniably good-looking: a smooth brown tan contrasted with the distinguished flecks of grey that were just beginning to show at the temples. His mouth tilted slightly in an upward curve on the left side. It was a mouth, Khavichev mused, which must fascinate women. But the man's most striking feature—like that of Khavichev—lay in his eyes: clear, ice-blue, and, in the film, laughing back at the camera.

For five minutes they sat silently watching the man posed against a series of recognisable London landmarks—gazing up the river from Westminster Bridge, strolling in Hyde Park, smiling in front of the London Hilton and leaning elegantly against the rails of Buckingham Palace. Finally, a set of close-ups—full-face; left and right profiles. The screen went blank and the lights came on again. One of the soldiers moved to draw the curtains. There was an uncomfortable tension in the room overlooking Red Square. At last Khavichev spoke.

"The subject of that film is especially susceptible to women. I need not tell you that the operative who took those shots risked her honour—and I might add, lost it. In the Dorchester Hotel, I believe. For security reasons her name now appears on the list of Honoured Artists of the Republic."

Nobody moved, Khavichev continued: "We have been looking at a member of the British Department of Special Security. His name is Brian Ian Oakes. He is between forty-five and forty-six years of age and is known to his intimates by the particularly nauseating nickname 'Boysie.' His code letter is 'L,' and for some considerable time he was the chief liquidating agent for Special Security. His record until last year showed him responsible for the deaths of at least twenty-five of our operatives."

Khavichev paused, looking at each of his Departmental Heads in turn. "But," he said, "information led us to believe that the man was not all he seemed. During the spring and early summer of last year we became increasingly certain that in reality the man was a neurotic dolt. There was even evidence that he did not carry out the liquidating operations himself."

Khavichev's voice assumed a cold harshness. "We were proved wrong. Mr Boysie Oakes showed himself to be a most painful thorn in our flesh during the bungled, miscalculated and totally inadequate 'Operation Coronet'* devised by Comrade Varlamov. You recall Mr Boysie Oakes, Comrade?"

Varlamov's face was a picture of suppressed fury: "I remember him, Comrade General." An undercurrent of venom beneath the smoothness.

"Good. Then watch that door." Khavichev raised his hand towards the door to the right of the screen. His left hand slid to the white button. The door opened and a man walked slowly into the space between the table and screen.

If the newcomer had been a naked freak, with two of everything, the effect of his appearance could not have been more startling. Varlamov half rose to his feet, his mouth forming a silent oath. The others froze—Archeyev in the act of lighting a cigarette, Porovsky with a hand to his head. The man who stood before Russia's Espionage High Command was, to all intents and purposes, Boysie Oakes—the one-time Liquidator for British Special Security.

"Amazing," purred the Director. "Mr Boysie Oakes to the life."

Varlamov allowed the oath to escape—loudly. Khavichev continued to smile.

"Just walk around for a moment, will you." He spoke to the man on display who smiled back, increasing the upward curve of his mouth's left corner. For a few moments he paraded for inspection by the quartet.

*For the terrifying facts surrounding " Operation Coronet " see *The Liquidator*.

"You may go." Khavichev dismissed him curtly and turned back to his brother officers.

"For your information only." Again there was the penetrating cut of authority. "We discovered this man quite by accident. Eight months ago he was a clerk in a tractor-works. Luckily for us, an intelligent clerk. In a few days he will have completed a rigorous course of training. He walks, talks, eats, and, I suspect, thinks like Mr Boysie Oakes. Our best linguists and our most competent instructors have worked on him continuously. He has been exposed to the latest methods of hypnotic and deep-sleep indoctrination. His real name is Vladimir Solev. Bearing in mind our friend Oakes' coding, I prefer to call him 'Double L'."

They had never really heard Khavichev laugh before. The cackle seemed to reach up from dark bowels to rumble out in a witch-like wheeze. The experience of hearing Khavichev laugh was not a pleasing one, thought Varlamov. The Director had controlled his mirth and was speaking again.

"I have not yet decided how, or when, we will use Solev. Oakes himself has been removed from his duties as Liquidator. At the moment he seems to be engaged in comparatively harmless courier work. But, my friends, I am certain that the time will come when we can perform a switch between Mr Oakes and Comrade Solev which will be to our lasting advantage."

He looked around almost benignly. "Good. Now to business. The change in plan is definitely on. London and Washington seem to have chosen an excellent date for their picnic, so we scrap our original Stage Three and concern ourselves with the new developments. I have been in touch with U-One—Gorilka —who tells me that the arrangements can be made without disturbing the original primary stages to any extent. Before we discuss the details of the unfortunate accident I would like to concentrate on the political repercussions as calculated against possible military outcome . . ."

The three Heads of Staff transferred their thoughts to the all-important work of the day—Stage Three of the complex operation which could possibly plant the most crippling blow yet into the hard solar plexus of the Western Alliance.

Outside in the sun, a big black party Zis saloon—with blinds drawn—was taking Vladimir Solev back to his private villa on the Lenin Hills near the University. There he would continue to polish his impersonation of Boysie Oakes.

I – CABLE

Miss Priscilla Braddock-Fairchild pulled on her midnight-blue lace briefs and ran her thumbs around the inside of the elastic to settle them firmly above her decorative hips. Sitting on the edge of the bunk she began to slide her stockings—Ballito Laceline—over neat calves and miraculous thighs. She looked down at Boysie who was far away, deep in unconscious Freudian exercises. The cabin walls shuddered to the steady thud of the ship's great single reduction geared turbines.

"Wake up, Boysie," whispered Miss Priscilla Braddock-Fairchild, bending over him and putting her lips close to his ear. "Wake up. I've got to get back to my own cabin. It's six o'clock." Boysie snuggled deeper into the pillow and groaned.

"Boysie, will you wake up!"

He opened one eye. The half-vision, bed's-eye-view of Miss Braddock-Fairchild thus provided caused him to snap up his other eyelid and shift his position with a sensual squirm.

"Har-Har!" gurgled Boysie Oakes lasciviously. "Gather round, me fine buckos."

"Oh no you don't. I'm sneaking back to my own cabin, darling. We dock at three and I've got to look reasonably wide awake when Daddy meets me." She was about to lift the gold evening sheath dress—discarded some four hours previously—over her jungle of jet hair. Boysie sighed as though resigned to the situation:

"So be it," he said, casually reaching out to a point just behind her tight knee.

An hour later, Miss Braddock-Fairchild dressed again and left the cabin. Boysie, now wide awake, lay back with hands laced behind his head, and revelled in the memory of Priscilla. They had met—one of those magnetic shipboard attractions—in the Caribbean Room, on the liner's first night out from Southampton five days before. She was a sultry, fine example of deflowered English maidenhood, and Boysie had reacted with the traditional ritualistic aplomb of the British man-about-ship. There had been martinis, gin and dancing; Bingo, smooching on the boat deck; more martinis—to the accompaniment of Sam Hawkins and his Trio in the Mermaid Bar—more gin, more dancing and, inevitably, by the second night, a delirious consummation—in Cabin B236: on the starboard side.

Boysie was content. Since he had returned from his last leave—to find that the Department of Special Security no longer required his services as their liquidating agent—the gigantic neuroses, which had for so long been the background pattern to his life, were gradually being sifted from the somewhat tangled skein of his personality. Mostyn, the Second-in-Command, hinted at possible dark assignments for the future; but, until now, Boysie had merely been entrusted with a handful of simple courier jobs. True, these had not always gone as smoothly as he would have liked. There was the case of the rocket fuel formula which had escaped his memory, necessitating an extra return journey to Berlin; and the terrible trouble over the NATO maps which he had inadvertently left in the lavatory of that little bistro opposite the Gare du Nord. Still, it was all in the game, thought Boysie. He wasn't the first agent to drop a ghoolie and, to be fair, both the Chief and Mostyn had been understanding.

Now, there would be one night in New York, to deliver new code corrections—slammed into his mind during a four-hour stint with Mostyn—then back on board the *Elizabeth* for the return trip. There would certainly be a counterpart to Miss Braddock-Fairchild on the eastward journey. Life was good; the *Elizabeth* was ploughing steadily towards the Ambrose lightship and the mouth of the Hudson.

But at this precise moment, while Boysie was ruminating on his good fortune, a cablegram was being received in the ship's radio room. The cablegram was addressed to Mr Brian Oakes and was, to say the least, a harbinger of chaos.

THE CABLEGRAM originated from the tall drab building, just off Whitehall, which served as clearing house and central head-quarters for Special Security. There, at about three-thirty on the previous afternoon, the Chief, having returned from a long and somewhat bibulous luncheon with a former Defence Minister at the *Athenaeum*, paced his office in a state of supreme irritation. Steady pacing was the Chief's favourite, and automatic, method for cooling fury; a habit devised long long ago when serving on the bridges of several of England's more indomitable warships.

The Chief had been striding—and regularly prodding at the direct-call bell which connected with Mostyn's office—for about five minutes before his Second-in-Command, short and suave as a high-class con man, arrived through the door at speed.

"You wanted me, sir?" Mostyn's voice rarely strayed from the smooth almost seductive tone of friendly menace.

"No, Mostyn. I'm just strengthenin' me bloody finger muscles for the Olympic Tiddlywinks Team."

"Very healthy exercise I'm told, sir." Mostyn usually knew just how far he could go with the Chief, but he quickly realised that the crusty old man was not in the jesting vein today.

"Where in the name of the Great Whore of Maida Vale have you been?" The strange oath came out coldly, lacking the warmth of true rage.

Mostyn had, in fact, been dallying with a charming member of the Royal Opera House chorus over a lunch of delicious subtlety at the *Tiberio*. He could normally handle the Chief when the mood was black. But this, he realised, was not just a black mood. It was a horrible combination of alcohol and Trouble—with a capital and tremolo T.

"Something up, sir?" His voice was level, but a tincture of concern plopped uneasily into the back of his mind. The Chief stopped pacing and faced Mostyn.

"Something up?" He repeated Mostyn's words as though they had been spoken in a dead language. It was unfortunate that his secretary chose that moment to tap at the door and enter with the afternoon tea tray.

"Your tea, sir."

The Chief's reply was not so much obscene as magnificently unprintable. In an admirable speech of some forty words he outlined half-a-dozen new, and hitherto untried, diversions which he suggested his secretary might try with teacup, saucer and three different brands of tea—including his own favourite Choice Rich Assam.

The secretary—a blonde whose bombshell had exploded several years previously—had been subjected to many such humiliating moments during her service with the top brass of Special Security. She stood passively holding the tray until the Chief stopped speaking.

"Here, or my office?" she asked, unsmiling.

"Go to hell!" said the Chief.

"Very good, sir."

The Chief made a mental note to buy her a dozen pairs of nylons in the morning.

In the silence which followed the secretary's departure Mostyn looked down at his elegantly-shod feet and noticed that there was a graze in the centre of the buffalo-hide toe cap of his left shoe. The Chief went over to the window and stared out at the steady stream of June rain which hissed upon London.

"What seems to be the matter, Chief?" Mostyn was the first to speak.

The Chief answered without turning from the window.

"Dudley's dead."

Mostyn opened his mouth, but no words came. The news had the surprise effect of an unexpected punch above the heart. For years he had known and liked Dudley—their Field Security Expert with the US High Command in Washington. In the old days they had worked together. Mostyn's stomach contracted. Dudley was about his age. Strange that, in a business where life was not particularly expensive, the death of a contemporary could give you that dreadful chill intimation of your own mortality.

"It's a bastard." The Chief's voice was unusually soft. Dudley had been one of his particular favourites.

Mostyn took a deep breath: "Accident or . . .?"

"Oh, accident." The Chief waved away any thought of underground enemy action. "Car smash—'automobile wreck' the long-winded twits called it. On Route 66 last night. He was on his way to San Diego. That's our stinkin' problem."

"San Diego?"

"San Diego. Gateway to Mexico. Home of the United States Pacific Fleet." The Chief turned and rested his fat buttocks against the window-sill. "And next week—in seven days' time —that is where they will be doin' the firin' trials with *Playboy.*"

"Oh!" Mostyn began to realise the implications.

"Yes. Bloody oh! Brand spankin' new atomic submarine, launchin' platform for the . . . the . . ." He paused, his mind feeling its way gingerly through a layer of alcohol. ". . . the . . . what's the name of the blasted weapon?"

"The *Trepholite.*"

"The Trephol-bloody-ite. Daft bleedin' name to give a missile."

"Biggest sea-to-ground-sea-to-air-sea-to-sea bang yet," murmured Mostyn: a simple statement of fact.

"So the damn Yanks say. Believe it when I see it." The Chief coughed, looked up and added hastily: "Not that I will be able to damn well see it. Can't possibly get away. Realise that, don't you?" His voice pleaded for Mostyn's confirmation of this last remark. The Chief did not like the United States, and those citizens of the United States who were forced into occasional contact with the Chief did not take well to him.

"Good gracious, no, sir. You can't possibly go," drawled the Second-in-Command, his voice taking on the calm velvet of reassurance. There was a three beats' silence.

"Spot of whisky?" said the Chief, his face settling into a satisfied smirk.

"Not at the moment, sir. Thanks all the same." Mostyn could have used a quart of whisky, but when the Chief was as tricky as this, it was better to keep the brain reasonably agile.

The Chief had the drinks cupboard—high behind his desk—half open. Mostyn hesitated for about five seconds after refusing the proffered spirits. Then, very quietly, with a sprinkle of grated cheese round the larynx. "I might add, sir, that I cannot go either. Far too much on the boil in Europe."

"Understood, me dear chap." The Chief was changing his tactics. "Quite understood. Wouldn't expect to turf you out of London at this time of the year—'cept for something of Top import. Sure you won't have a snort?" He was slopping himself a large Chivas Regal.

"Quite sure." Mostyn shut his mouth firmly in a tight smile on the word 'sure'.

"Trouble is," said the Chief dropping into his swivel chair, and taking a long pull at his drink, "trouble is, who, by all the holy monks of great renown, is going to go?"

"Who indeed?" said Mostyn benignly.

The Chief sighed. "There's the bleedin' rub, as the Bard has it. Got to be an experienced operational officer, FO5*: that's essential—treaty instructions and all that cock." There was another short pause. Mostyn felt an aura of danger pass between them. The Chief looked up at him from under those great brows—once the scourge of many a gunroom. "Took the liberty of checkin' your operational list, old man. Bit thin on the ground, aren't you?"

"Suppose we are, sir. But the new continual surveillance on Cabinet Ministers—since *Operation Keelroll*—takes a fair slice of my boys. . . ."

"I'm not criticisin'." The Chief cut in with the right hand raised pontifically and voice spiked with a pipette load of acid. They looked at one another, the space between throbbing a checkmate atmosphere.

At last Mostyn found himself being stared out. He shifted his

*FO5 : Foreign Office 5. Security clearance from the Foreign Office runs from —1 down to —8 ; and from 1 to 8. FO5 is generally high rating. FO6, 7 and 8 are for VIP Security Top Brass only.

gaze back to the blemish on his buffalo-hide. A minute slid by unseen and unheard.

"There is just one possibility . . ." he began; then, with a sharp and definitive change of mind, continued, "No! No! No! No, that wouldn't really do."

He started to pace up and down: an effete facsimile of his superior. The Chief was getting irritated again; his clenched fist pounding the desk top to a slow steady rhythm.

"Come on, Mostyn. What's on your mind? We're pushed, laddie, and the old grey matter's not functioning as smoothly as it might." He swallowed the remainder of his whisky in an enormous gulp and leaned over the desk. "If we do not have someone on the Official Observer's list for next week, the Ministry might start askin' questions about our strength. Maybe the Treasury will have a go as well. Think where that could land us."

Mostyn thought—quickly. The idea of the Treasury poking their serrated gold beaks into the internal finances of the Department was enough to bring even Mostyn heavily up against the true heart of the matter. He took a deep breath and began to blurt, somewhat pompously:

" 'L' will be in New York tomorrow: delivering the July code corrections. But it's ridiculous, he doesn't know a conning tower from a cowslip . . ."

"Aren't called conning towers any more. Not in nuclear submarines," said the Chief sharply. "Called sails. Anyway, shouldn't have really thought it mattered if he couldn't tell a Wren's brassière from a quarantine flag. Thing is, he's an experienced operator. Don't see why we can't use him."

"Oh, Boysie's all right," said Mostyn uncertainly. "Only, well, you know he's inclined to be on the careless side."

"Good great Nelson's braces, the fella's only got to sit in a fornicatin' submarine and look at a pulsatin' radar screen."

"He'll have to write a report."

"You can help 'im with that, can't you? Blast it, fly 'im back here as soon as it's all over. He tells you what he saw and you put it in the right lingo. Damn it man, he's a godsend. Probably

25

get on with the Yanks like a pig in a mire. Can't understand why you've lost faith in the bloke. Saved all our bacon with the *Coronet* thing."

"Well . . ." Mostyn's mind had subsided into a picture of Boysie full fathom five behind the armoured hull of a nuclear submarine. When you knew Boysie you were naturally conscious of the hundred and one things that could go wrong. The dream progressed with astonishing rapidity. Now Boysie had got up from his radar screen to be sick, or pee, or something; his hand had accidentally touched a button, and the *Trepholite* had gone blazing up out of the blue Pacific to land flaming on New York—in the rush hour. Mostyn was beginning to sweat. Why was it that Boysie always did this to him? It was bad enough in the old days, but since that last bit of trouble even the most simple job given to Boysie brought Mostyn out in the singing terrors.

The Chief sliced cleanly into the daymare: "Gettin' nowhere, so I'm goin' to give you a direct order. 'L' is over there. Right? If 'L' don't go on to San Diego as our bleedin' observer, then I shall have to send you. Right?"

Mostyn groaned internally, "As you say, sir. Right." His intuition told him that neither this day nor those immediately following were going to be particularly good. "I'll set up a contact for briefing in New York and cable San Diego and Boysie," he said wearily. "I expect they'll arrange for a courier to take him down there. But if he does manage to louse it up, then I'm not going to take the responsibility. This is being done under your direct orders, sir."

"Ah!" said the Chief. "Where's that fat-arsed girl with the tea?"

As Mostyn got to the door, the Chief called out, "Do me a favour, will you." Mostyn turned. The Chief was looking suddenly older and his bright little eyes were strangely watery. "Fix up a wreath for Dudley," said the Chief quietly. The two men looked at one another in mutual understanding. Mostyn nodded and went out.

BACK IN his office, Mostyn pressed the buzzer for his secretary, ordered tea, and sent her down for the photostats of Dudley's briefing for the *Playboy* firing trials. The documents ran into six foolscap pages of opaque jargon, from which the Second-in-Command gleaned nothing fresh about America's latest nuclear-powered launching pad. From the statistics at the end of her sea trials, *Playboy* was very fast and, on paper, an admirable ramp for the *Trepholite*—a missile about which there were no statistics, only rumours carried back and forth by worried-looking Naval Attachés. And if these ruddy-faced, preoccupied young men from the Admiralty were anything to go by (Mostyn contemplated), the *Trepholite* was the supreme deterrent. Literally the last word. So the firing trials from its undersea emplacement were of considerable importance to everyone's peace of mind.

The final page outlined the duties of Special Security's observer, and with it came hope. Boysie would be one of eight experts—and inexperts—who had to sit sober on board *Playboy* while the Weapons Officer lit the blue touch paper (metaphorically speaking). It was also heartening to see that the *Trepholite* would be fired "cold"—without its holocaustic warhead. Perhaps the Chief was right. Even though this was far from Boysie's usual line of country, he couldn't really get into any trouble. As for the report, well the American boys would feed him a certain amount of data and, if the worst came to the worst, the Department could, with a little subtle persuasion, always get their grubby hands on a copy of the Admiralty observer's report before Boysie wrote his. The important thing was they should have someone from the Department actually there in the flesh; and, whatever else you could say about Boysie, he was very expert in the flesh.

An hour later, Mostyn came to the conclusion that Boysie's presence in San Diego would simply be nominal. A couple of quick gins at the club on his way home should soon dispel the tiny lone butterfly that fluttered angrily at the back of Mostyn's conscience. Again he buzzed his secretary, and began to fill in a set of cablegram forms: one to the Chief of US Naval Security, North Island, San Diego; one to his opposite number at the

Pentagon; one to their undercover man in New York (a personality unknown to all departments of US Intelligence, including the CIA. Such is the trust of allies): and one to Mr Brian Oakes, passenger on board the *Queen Elizabeth*. Mostyn sealed each of the buff forms in a separate envelope, initialled them and added the requisite code designations. The first two were marked *Top Sec A*; the latter couple *Sub-Text: Normal*.

His secretary, a bouncily efficient girl with undisguised false breasts, carried the forms up to the top floor and handed them to the Duty Cypher Officer. In the Cypher Room—where, behind double metal doors, Britain's secrets and clandestine orders are filtered out in a jumble of letters—the daughter of a retired Major-General translated Mostyn's scrawl into the required coding series. Boysie's cablegram remained almost as Mostyn had written it:

RETURN PASSAGE POSTPONED STOP DELIVER ORDER AND
AWAIT FURTHER INSTRUCTIONS REFERENCE OPENING NEW
SALES AREA STOP BRANCH MANAGER TO CALL AT YOUR HOTEL
STOP DO NOT ACKNOWLEDGE STOP REGARDS UNCLE

Boysie's cablegram was handed to one of the trainee cypher operators. He left the building ten minutes later and within half an hour telephoned the message through the ordinary GPO channels from a Paddington number. Boysie's instructions were off on their journey to the *Queen Elizabeth's* radio room. On arrival, the cablegram lay in the delivery tray—with seven other freshly-received personal messages—for half an hour before being popped into its little crested envelope and hurried down to Cabin B236. From the moment it left Mostyn's hand to the time Boysie hurriedly tore it open at least twelve people had seen its contents.

THEY GOT Khavichev out of bed around two-thirty in the morning. He gave three sets of orders over the scrambler telephone in his night office and went back to bed. The time had come and it could not have happened at a more judicious moment. Tomorrow there would be much to do. The organisation had to be foolproof.

JUST BEFORE they woke him, in the villa on the outskirts of the city. Vladimir Solev had been dreaming of the dark Ukrainian girl who had been his guest on the previous evening. At first he thought it was her hand on his shoulder, shaking him up from the warmth of sleep. But it was his staff instructor. He was to be in the briefing room in one hour. He would be going on a journey and there would be further orders on arrival. The situation—his instructor told him, sitting on the bed like a sick visitor—was fluid. But there was little doubt that the training was going to be put to the test. His glorious moment would soon come.

Vladimir Solev—Boysie Oakes' double—felt his stomach rise. He heaved noisily, and quite effectively, into his handkerchief.

BOYSIE READ the cablegram twice. Once, standing by the wash basin, where he had just been completing his morning shave when the steward arrived with the white envelope on a silver tray. Again, slumped—a quivering, boneless jelly—in his armchair after croaking "No reply" in the wake of the departing flunkey. Boysie could understand why those Old Testament kings used to exterminate bearers of bad tidings. He had taken an almost homicidal dislike to the wretched man who had delivered this Boysie-changing slip of paper.

Unlike Solev, Boysie had no use for his handkerchief. For ten minutes he retched out his fear into the basin—moaning in anguish and accidentally upsetting a bottle of *Floris 89* toilet water on to the cabin floor where it left a damp circle of fragrance which later caused the cabin steward to raise his eyebrows a little higher than usual. Boysie had not felt like this for months. His hands were shaking; his bowels seemed to contain a small electric mixer, turned to top speed and operating a dough hook; his heart was thudding audibly under the sea island cotton vest; and his throat felt as though someone was titillating his uvula with a cotton-wool swab.

He was all too familiar with the symptoms. The diagnosis was simple—stark, staring, yellow fear in a massive overdose. In the months that had passed since the Chief—via Mostyn—had taken him off the liquidating assignments, Boysie had never really allowed himself to think about possible reactions to any dangerous operation that the Department might put in his way. Life had been quiet, gay and good. Boysie had felt that if Mostyn ever came up with a diabolical scheme that was beyond his small, nervous, neurotic powers, he could always spin a neat excuse from his cunning mind and so slide out of the Department for good and all.

But now it was here. Right out of the cloudless blue, the dark business of having to work near death had caught him unawares. There was no mistaking the cablegram. It could mean one thing only. An operation, of some kind, was brewing. An operation earmarked specially for Boysie. And Boysie knew, through bitter experience, that in the Department operations were dangerous. Blue funking dangerous. For the hundredth time since he had been eased into the Department, Boysie wondered how he had managed to get mixed up in the game at all.

"Bloody hell!" he groaned to himself. "Oh bloody, bloody hell. Why didn't I get out of it after the last little lot?" He looked blankly round the cabin which seemed despicably normal. The old cry of fear was ripping him apart: and he did not even know what the operation was. BRANCH MANAGER TO CALL AT YOUR HOTEL contained the key to unknown terrors. Boysie's mind started to dwell deeply on the possibilities. He might easily be left waiting for this "Branch Manager" for a week or two—Mostyn had always been an inconsiderate bastard —and, to be left cooling one's heels would only increase the nervous tension. A myriad pictures weaved through Boysie's pregnant imagination. He saw himself being shot at by hulking great men in slouch hats and raincoats; chased over scaffolding, mountain high above the city; roped and gagged in a cellar crawling with puce spiders (at the very thought of spiders, Boysie was attacked by what looked like the rectangular twitch); pushed into a swimming bath containing a red-eyed octopus; and put to the torture by a voluptuous negress. He lingered over this last, for the negress turned out to be a diverting girl. At least it was a sign that the initial impact of fear was passing. Slowly, Boysie began turning his mind from the horrors. In their place stood the short, compact, oily, curly-haired figure of Mostyn—his immediate boss. In times of stress Boysie always took comfort in railing silently upon Mostyn. Now he railed—with a selection of oaths and curses that would not have disgraced a joint meeting of Macbeth's Witches and the most proficient members of the Billingsgate Bad Language League.

A few hours, and six brandies, later, Boysie stood—still in a profound state of anxiety—on the games deck. He leaned moodily against the rail, crowded with passengers eager for their first glimpse of the Manhattan skyline. Away to the left, the Statue of Liberty raised a green hand, half-aggressive, half-pleading. Boysie smiled for the first time since the cablegram had arrived. "Please, miss, can I leave the sea?" he muttered to himself, watching the statue's suppliant arm slide past.

Downtown Manhattan came up, rusty and grey mixed with heat-haze. The dogmatic wail of a police siren floated over the water from the West Side Highway. Up river they could see the slim skyscrapers, climbing pock-marked fingers. A broad American with watery eyes and a purple checked jacket nudged Boysie hard in the ribs and pointed to the centre of the forest of concrete peaks:

"There it is, bud. Biggest phallic symbol in the world. The good old Empire State."

Boysie could see the man's point. Even at this distance, he thought, New York looked as sexy as he had always been led to believe.

Forty-five minutes later he stood sweating in the queue which moved, almost imperceptibly, into the main lounge, where US immigration officials sat impassively scrutinising passports. In spite of his light linen suit, voile shirt and tropical underwear. Boysie felt as though he was sitting, wrapped round with rugs, in a Turkish bath. The heat seemed to claw into his skin, wrenching the drops of perspiration from the pores by force. By the time he reached the head of the queue, Boysie felt so tired—a by-product of emotional fatigue and the strength-sapping heat—that he had consciously ceased to worry about the immediate future. His imagination was brimful of ice cubes slowly melting in a tall drink, and the exquisite chill of a cold shower, followed by soft breezes fluttering over his body, emanating from fans—preferably wielded by silk-thighed Vargas-girls.

An aquiline immigration man, with the name 'Gozinsky' stencilled on to a circular plastic disc pinned to the left side of his brown uniform shirt, quietly took Boysie's passport and opened it.

"Mr Oakes?" he asked without looking up.

"Yes."

Gozinsky turned away, and with an almost invisible nod caught the eye of a squat, leather-faced little man who had been sprawling in one of the main lounge arm-chairs a few feet away. The man toddled over to the immigration table.

"Yours, Joe," said Gozinsky.

"Oakes?" said Joe.

Gozinsky cocked his head towards Boysie, at the same time going through the prestidigital exercise of stamping the passport, flicking it back into Boysie's wilting palm and saying: "Welcome to New York. Welcome to the United States. Mr Siedler here has been waiting for you."

Mr Siedler came forward, his chubby face breaking into an outsize smile. Big welcoming smiles were Joe Siedler's speciality. At one time—when he had worked as a CIA trigger man —they had been of great use to him. Those were the days when Joe Siedler's friendly smile was often the last thing his clients ever saw. "I guess they rest easier if you give it 'em kinda friendly like," he used to say. "You just goes up, puts out your hand, turns on the pearlies and says, 'Howdy'. They're at ease.

Relaxed. Like comfortable. Then whammy-whammy with the old thirty-two, and mutton. That's the way it goes." But Joe Siedler's operational days were now long over, and his professionalism had been turned to escorting couriers and special VIP agents. This one was just routine, but Siedler still put everything he had into the act.

"Brian Oakes? Gee, am I glad to see you." He came round the table exuding a glow of good fellowship. Boysie's reaction was standard. He began to feel wanted again. In contact. Among friends. Siedler's hand was firm in his, and his arm was being pumped as though the American expected oil to gush out of his ears.

"Geez, it's hot, Mr Oakes, let's get off this floating greenhouse, hunh? How much luggage you got?"

"Only this case." Boysie lugged up the heavy tan Revelation with which he always travelled, and allowed himself to be led out of the main lounge, into the lift that dropped them to A Deck, across the foyer and down the gangway—all to the accompaniment of a stream of friendly chatter:

"My name's Siedler, Mr Oakes, Joe Siedler—call me Joe, everyone does. Your first time in New York? Yeah? It is? Great. Well, you're gonna like it here. Nowhere in the world like New York. We gotta dandy room fixed up for you at the New Weston over on Madison and 50th. You'll like the New Weston: lots of Limeys stay there. They got a tea parlour and all. One of our boys'll be over to see you in about an hour. Plenty o' time for you to freshen up. You'll be real comfortable. You sure I can't carry that bag of yours, looks mighty heavy to me? No? Well, you know best, Mr Oakes—or can I call you Brian?"

"My friends call me Boysie."

"Boysie? Hey whaddya know? No kidding? What kinda funny name is that, hunh? Boysie? Great, hunh? Greata know you, Boysie. Look, we gotta get that bag cleared by customs. Sure is nice havin' you here."

They reached the foot of the gangway and pushed their way through the chaos which thronged Pier 90. Boysie caught sight

3   33

of Priscilla Braddock-Fairchild looking lost, surrounded by a hillock of cream luggage. Through the whole of the closed customs area of the pier, passengers were scavenging for their cases, trunks and hat boxes which were being expelled from the ship's side—rolling off the conveyor belts like so much waste. The strange inferno-like scene was being superintended by a covey of bored-looking customs men, their disinterested manner belying that sharp awareness which could be detected, by the perceptive, at ten paces. Siedler elbowed his way past a frantic skinny and blue-rinsed lady who was yapping shrewishly at her distraught spouse: "Well, go and ask someone, you dumb cluck. The box must be somewhere."

Boysie, keeping as close as possible to Siedler, saw his escort approach a uniformed customs man who was passing the time by carrying out a carefully detailed inspection of the end of a much-chewed cigar. Sielder's lips moved and his hand came up with an identity badge. The cigar-chewer nodded. By this time Boysie had reached them.

"This is the guy," said Siedler happily.

"O.K. This the only bag you got, mister?"

"Just the one."

"O.K." The operation was painless.

With a little pink customs label slapped tight to the Revelation they tramped the length of the pier—past a hundred tiny human dramas, each coming to its climax at the end of the Atlantic crossing—and out into the equally chaotic street where about fifty people seemed to be fighting to commandeer four taxis. Siedler led Boysie across the street, under the West Side Highway, to a long black Cadillac which stood purring sweetly by the kerb. A coloured chauffeur ambled pleasantly round to the rear door and took Boysie's case.

"This is her, Boysie buddy. Sweet job, hunh?" said the beaming Siedler. "Avallon will take your bag, then we'll hit the road."

AMONG THE crowd watching the disembarkation from Pier 90 was a cadaverous youth, known to his intimates as

34

Skull Face—for the obvious reason that he could, with ease, have played Yorick for the Royal, or any other, Shakespeare Company. For the best part of two hours Skull Face had stood, his deep-set eyes fixed on the exit gates. As the customs-cleared passengers began to filter out on to the steaming dock-side, the lad started to make a careful examination of each face. Skull Face had a good eye when it came to spotting people. Boysie and the rosy Siedler were easily identifiable. There was no need for a second look. In a matter of seconds Skull Face was inside a telephone booth, dialling the number of a night club in the East 70s.

"He got here," said Skull Face when the familiar voice answered.

"Good boy. Thank you. I won't forget you, kid. See you around."

"Thanks," said Skull Face. "See ya, boss."

CHICORY TRIPLEHOUSE was naked and twenty-five years old. She lay, bored and very erotic, on the silk bedcover which enveloped the wide divan—central piece of furniture, and focal point, of her bedroom high over Park Avenue. When dressed, Chicory Triplehouse was stunning; naked, she defied description. Her body was an overall deep gold—a smooth tan which indicated that she sunbathed only in the altogether; a tan which displayed none of the tell-tale white patches over the bra and pantie areas of her spectacular flesh. The only slight discolouration on the gorgeous body was an area of about four square inches a shade darker on the right thigh—a birthmark in the shape of a perfect heart.

She shifted, languidly, on to her left side, reaching out for the pack of Kents on the bedside table. The movement altered her contours. From her right ankle the line swept up in a grand ellipse over her rising thigh and hip, then flattened to the firm half globe of her breast and curved to the slim long neck. Lazily she brushed away a lock of tawny hair which had fallen across her face, lit a cigarette, and lay back, opening her lips to expel the grey straggle of smoke.

Chicory sighed, moving her shoulders and buttocks against the silk, feeling it soft on her skin. Quarter of an hour before, she had put a random pile of records on to the player. Now the music had started to penetrate her consciousness, where, before, it had been mere background. Les Swingle Singers were do-daddle-daing through their far-out rendition of the *Sinfonia* from Bach's *Partita No. 2*. The sad, long solo of the female voice (the best moment of the record) was suddenly turned sour by the off-key trang of the white bedside telephone.

"Hallo," said Chicory Triplehouse, her voice husky against the music which still bopped on from the record player.

"Chicky, my darling girl." The accent was a shade too English, a morsel over-patronising. But Chicory, who was very susceptible to voices, could, by closing her eyes, immediately bring to mind the smell of the man far away at the other end of the wire—the clean tang of the healthy male, the odour of good grooming, helped on by a hint of *Mark II* after-shower lotion.

"My favourite Englishman. Darling, where are you? Can't you come over? I'm feeling lonesome."

"Actually, old girl, I was hoping you'd come over and see me."

"Oh?"

"Are you as bored as ever?"

"Naturally, honey."

"Well, we'll soon change all that. How about a little trip to Cal-if-orn-aye-eh?"

"You mean it? For real."

"Got a job for you. Helping a poor lonely Englishman across this great big dusty country of yours."

"Is it to do with your work?"

"Yes. Always said that I'd find something interesting in it for you. All expenses paid."

"And who's the poor lonely Englishman?"

" 'Fraid it's not me, my love. But I assure you that he's scrumptious."

"I'll be right over. Just hold him for me." She had put down the receiver and was rummaging among a froth of wispy nylon in the wardrobe drawer before her gentleman caller had time to reply.

IN THE back room which served as a manager's office for the *Club Fondante* in the East 70s, two burly men, who both appeared to have given up the fight game a dozen bouts too late, stood looking down at a freshly developed photograph of Boysie Oakes. The third member of the party, a tall iron-grey man whose name was Cirio, leaned across the desk and spoke.

"The orders aren't as full or precise as I would have liked. But I guess they can only mean the guy has to be picked up and brought over here—quietly and efficiently. That means no blasting and no witnesses. I don't want anything in the newspapers either. Got it?"

"OK, we'll fix it," said the first hoodlum.

"Yea, we'll fix it good. Like so quiet he'll think he's been shuttled here on a magic carpet," echoed the second.

CHICORY TRIPLEHOUSE, looking like a fashion plate, came out of the apartment building on Park Avenue. The doorman hailed a cab and she drove off to an address in Greenwich Village.

COMFORTABLE IN a big fan-jet on direct flight from New York to San Diego, Priscilla Braddock-Fairchild looked at the weathered profile of her father, Commander Braddock-Fairchild, RN, who was snoring away the cloud-scaped miles. Miss Braddock-Fairchild leaned back, closed her eyes and tightened her thigh muscles. A smile of pleasure flickered over her face. She was thinking about Boysie Oakes.

THE TU104 may not be the most comfortable aircraft in the world, but, like most things Russian, it exudes a firm, if stark, utilitarian dependability. TU104 USSR42400 had started its flight from Sheremetyevo Airport, Moscow. Now it turned on the downwind leg of its final approach—the dive brakes coming out with that unique and distinctive power-drill sound. Below, divided Berlin lay in twinkling silence. Vladimir Solev, the first part of his journey almost completed, tried to drag his mind away from the possibility of the airliner plunging out of control into the ground. Solev was finding it hard to resign himself to the inevitable consequences of fate. In less than two hours he would be boarding another aeroplane. This time a capitalist aeroplane bound for New York. Vladimir Solev felt miserable. He was thinking about Boysie Oakes.

JAMES GEORGE MOSTYN, Second-in-Command of British Special Security, woke in a cold sweat at five minutes past four in the morning. He reached across the bed and remembered that he was alone. The charming lady from the Royal Opera House chorus had apologised, but uttered a firm "No."

Mostyn's intuition was playing tricks again. On the face of things there was nothing to worry about. But the situation into which he had plunged Boysie reeked uncomfortably of normality. James George Mostyn shivered. He was thinking about Boysie Oakes.

IN THE War Room of Soviet Counter-Espionage the orders were being transmitted. Khavichev himself had roughed out the amendments to the plan. They had been coded and sent off to New York, San Diego and London, with copies to all heads of departments.

The operation had begun. Khavichev was lighthearted. An unexpected move by the British had placed a dazzling opportunity in his way. Khavichev smiled—the look of a wolf tasting blood. He was thinking about Boysie Oakes.

IN NEW YORK and San Diego the pawns were being drawn together, invisibly moved into each other's orbits by the cold, uncompromising hands of British Special Security and Soviet Counter-Espionage and Subversive Activities.

II – CHICORY

BOYSIE was feeling considerably better. He stepped out of the shower and towelled himself vigorously—the external tingle supplemented by an internal glow and sense of well-being induced by two stiff Old Hickory Bourbons with which he had sluiced out his throat shortly after arriving at the hotel.

The journey from Pier 90 had been a travelogue in miniature—Joe Siedler rattling off facts; acquainting Boysie with landmarks in a stream of Runyonese which was almost as baffling as the swirling racket of the city at high pitch. To Boysie, New York became, in the first few minutes, a noisy, terrifying, wild brake-slamming fairground—garish, with the harsh compelling beauty of luxury-stressed concrete, steel and glass thrown in.

It was in the hotel lobby, while Siedler was doing his usual incomparable liaison job with the management, that Boysie committed his first transatlantic blunder. Realising that, in his state of mental deshabille on leaving the ship, he had forgotten to arm himself with a duty-free ration of cigarettes, he approached the booth—which, loaded with newspapers, magazines, gum and potential clouds of nicotine smoke, is standard equipment in hotels the world over—and looked among the choice selection for his favourite brand of Benson and Hedges King-size Filters. Not seeing them, he caught the eye of the vendor and automatically asked for "Twenty *Players*, please."

"Twenty what?" said the laconic booth-minder.

"Players," repeated Boysie, sounding like a television ad.

"Sure, Mac. What kindya want? Football or baseball?"

Boysie eventually settled for Chesterfields, plonked himself into one of the leather armchairs (which seemed to have been provided for middle-aged gentlemen waiting for sleek young girls, and middle-aged ladies waiting for sleek young men), and lit a cigarette with the Windmaster which bore his unfortunate initials, B.O. The first lungful of smoke set him coughing, provoking shocked glances akin to those flung at people who talk in the reading rooms of public libraries.

Snippets of conversation buzzed round like midsummer bees; ". . . and she had this rather delightful Mercedes Benz. Milton and I met her in Europe last Fall . . ." ". . . You know, honey, he's very anxious to leave his wife. Did you know that? . . ." Then Siedler was back again, still beaming and bulging with fulsome bonhomie. During his negotiations he had collected an elderly bell-boy who now took Boysie's case and led them to the elevator in a manner suggesting that he did not really have to offer this menial service but was doing it out of respect for Anglo-American relations. The elevator whipped them up to the sixth floor, leaving Boysie's guts somewhere slightly below pavement level.

The room was large, with furnishings to match. A chest-of-drawers—surmounted by two huge candlestick lamps—ranged over the length of one wall; the bed could have slept three assorted couples, with room to spare for acrobatics; and the television, elegantly slim, might have been built for Cinerama. Siedler produced the Old Hickory ("Little welcome gift from the boys"), and lounged on the bed while Boysie unpacked to the whisper of the air conditioning.

A tap at the door announced the arrival of the CIA contact —a reserved young man in the uniform light grey suit of the American business executive, and the damp manner of one who has lost his sense of humour during the climb towards responsibility. He was introduced, rather soberly, as Mr Lofrese —Siedler's bouncy attitude changing noticeably to distinct deference in the presence of a senior member of his firm. There was an uncomfortable pause, after which Joe Siedler quietly took his leave, priming Boysie with two telephone numbers written in vermilion ink on the back of an old envelope.

"If you want anything, just call," was his final injunction. "If I ain't at this one, then try this—it's direct line to our Department. They'll always find me."

Lofrese set straight to business. Half an hour later Boysie's initial mission was completed—the code corrections noted carefully in a small, black leather-bound book, gold-embossed with the American eagle. "It's a wonder it hasn't got *Codes. Secret* stamped all over it," reflected Boysie.

"OK. That seems to be it, Mr Oakes." Lofrese's voice was reminiscent of an airport controller doing a GCA. Boysie wondered if he was really a computer in disguise, being operated by some remote automaton at Cape Kennedy. Boysie lit a cigarette and relaxed that tiny part of his mind which had been retaining the code corrections for over a week. But, with Lofrese's next words, his mind—together with all his senses, and accompanied by a quick downward pressure of the bowels —flicked into life again.

"I've got some instructions for you," said Lofrese. "Guess you've already been notified that you're staying on in the States for a while."

Boysie nodded, his heart pounding. Here it comes, he thought; the Sunday punch; Mostyn's little knife-thrust; the black one that he had dreaded. The least he expected was a directive to eliminate the whole of the Unites States High Command—single handed and armed only with a Boy Scout knife. He dragged his thoughts back to Lofrese who was speaking again:

"You're going out to San Diego, California, tomorrow. Like it out there, real nice."

"And what," said Boysie wrestling with the nervous tremor in his voice, "have I got to do in San Diego?"

"Sit in the sun . . ."

"For how long?"

". . . and watch a missile being fired from a submarine. Be out there about a week."

Oh no! It can't be as easy as that, thought Boysie.

But, when Lofrese had outlined the role of Britain's Special

Security observer for the *Playboy-Trepholite* firing trials, the anxieties started to filter away. This, Boysie considered, was beginning to look like a piece of cake—sponge, with chocolate and vanilla icing thrown in. San Diego was a magic name around which he could spin pictures of soft white sand and cream foam from the Pacific; of balmy evenings with Mexican music prodding him towards some curvaceous starlet on vacation from Hollywood only a hundred miles up the road. Today was Tuesday. The firing trials—Lofrese told him—were fixed for next Monday afternoon. Presumably they would have to spend one day being briefed for the event, but that would still leave him roughly four days of suntan, sand, swaying palms and a taste of the fabulous playground coast of California.

"How do I get there?"

"Fly presumably." (Boysie's stomach did a smart about-turn. Flying was his least favourite pastime.) Lofrese was still talking: "I am only instructed to pass on the nature of your duty. Your Department has just sent us another cable to say that they'll take care of you until your arrival in San Diego. I expect you'll get a call from one of your own people. Probably send someone down there with you. But when you do get there you are to report to your Royal Naval liaison officer at our base on North Island. Name of Braddock-Fairchild. Commander Braddock-Fairchild."

Boysie's eyes sparkled, and he distinctly felt a mink-clad hand move deliciously over his abdomen. Of course—his whole being was enveloped in a happy blush of pleasure—the passionate Priscilla's Old Man. She had said that "Daddy was stationed in California." Oh boy, breathed Boysie, are we going to commingle.

Now (forty-five minutes after Lofrese had left) completing the operation of drying himself following the shower. Boysie was alone and happy. Stripped, he padded over to the television and spent some time mastering the switches. One channel was showing a *Maverick* episode he had already seen in London; another, the original Wallace Beery version of *Treasure Island*; a third was entertaining the admass with a young-looking Olivier smoothing himself through *Rebecca*. Boysie began to hum "On the Road to Mandalay." The best picture came from a station intent on wiping out the entire US 5th Cavalry. Anyway, the Indians were really whooping it up before riding off over the skyline, getting into their big Thunderbirds and driving away to Beverly Hills. Boysie watched the carnage with one eye as he prepared to put on the white BD nylon shirt, dark Italian silk tie with the diamond dot motif, and the Swedish Terylene slim-line navyat suit he had laid out on the bed before taking his shower. He paused for a moment in front of the wall mirror to take a conceited peep at his figure. The television erupted in a splurge of hard-sell advertising. "Ladies," said Boysie in his dark-brown voice, "are your husbands lustless?" The telephone tringed as though in answer.

"Hallo," said Boysie into the receiver, thinking that this was not a very imaginative opening to his first telephone conversation in the New World.

" 'L'?" asked an English voice.

"Yes. 'L' here."

"Good. This is *USS One*."

"Oh!" said Boysie who could never remember the individual code classifications. There were times when he even had trouble with his own single letter. "Oh! That's nice."

"You've had your CIA instructions?"

"Yes. I'm waiting here now. They said my own people would be in touch."

"I am your own people, that's why I'm ringing." The voice lingered on the edge of impatience. "Number Two has been on to me. Asked me to find you a travelling companion to help you get to San Diego tomorrow. Less conspicuous than going alone. She'll be right over. Safe enough, but as far as she's concerned you're just a business man who wants to be shown the ropes and have his hand held. Got it?"

"I think so."

"Better to have someone quite unconnected with the Department, don't you think? Not that you're likely to have any trouble."

"No! Er . . . Yes, I agree," said Boysie, wondering what the hell the bloke was on about.

"OK. She knows you by your real name and has my number if you do happen to need me. I'm off to the *Coconut Grove*. Have a ball—as the cannibal chief said at the banquet." The line went dead. Boysie stood looking at the telephone. "Coconut Grove: Schmoconut Grove," he muttered. Finally he shrugged, placed the receiver back in its cradle, and began to dress.

He had got as far as the trousers, shirt and tie, and was reflecting on the age, colour of hair and eyes, and vital statistics of his travelling companion, when a double rap at the door announced company. Boysie did a quick neck bend in front of the mirror, rolling up his eyes to see that his hair was in place; then, touching his fingertips with his tongue and smoothing out his eyebrows, he switched on his charm-smile and opened the door. Two ape-type men were leaning against the corridor wall; both identically dressed in blue lightweight suits and snappy straw hats which would have looked better on Sinatra.

"Joe sent us," said the first ape, whose distinguishing marks included a large crescent scar below the right eye.

"Joe asked us to come over," said the second, following his companion past Boysie and into the room. "Sure gotta nice place up here. Classy."

"Joe who?" asked Boysie, leaving the door open and experiencing a mild palpitation of fear.

"Siedler. Who else?" said the man with the scar.

"Joe Siedler," echoed the other who, to Boysie's alarm, had never moved his hand from the inside of his jacket since entering the room.

"He didn't call," said Boysie with his back still to the open door. "What's he want, anyway?"

"Said we should take ya over to his place. Ya know, kinda celebration party. Shoot some craps, play a little pinochle, make with the booze, knock off a couple of broads."

Boysie was worried. He was not the quickest of men when it came to being on the uptake, but this did not sound like Siedler.

Come to think of it, it was more like an old Cagney movie—he could swear that he had seen both these characters before, in a myriad gangster films back in the 30s. Boysie took a deep breath:

"'Fraid you'll have to tell Joe I can't make it tonight. Got a date," he said, trying to sound nonchalant.

"Look, buddy." The hard rasp of intimidation had crept into the first ape's voice. "We don't want no trouble. Joe said to bring ya, so ya come over nice and quiet like. Hunh?"

Boysie's mind was doing a hundred yards sprint. He had been in New York for only a few hours and already the natives were looking ugly. He could feel his palms begin to film over with sweat, and that nasty trembling of the thigh muscles had set in. He took a pace forward.

"OK." A thin smile. "Don't you worry about it. I'll call Joe now, and tell him myself."

"Oh no you . . . !" The first man's hand shot out. Boysie instinctively sidestepped and made a lucky lunge towards the outstretched arm, catching it just above the wrist. Reacting automatically to the long training he had endured when Mostyn first pressed him into the service with the Department, Boysie pulled down hard on the arm, then jerked outwards and upwards, ducking under the armpit, and twisting the limb up behind the ape's back. At the same time he lifted his right knee, placing it above his opponent's buttocks. There was a painful wrenching noise. Putting all his weight behind the push, Boysie sent the stocky figure bumping through the open doorway.

"Ouroughoawl!" said the man loudly as he hit the corridor wall. At the same moment, Boysie felt a numbing flash of pain in his left shoulder. The other assailant had come from behind. There was a shout from outside, and the last thing Boysie remembered was a vision of blue and white with a tumble of yellow-brown hair framed in the doorway. Then a scream and the sound of hurrying footsteps. After that, a starless night closed around Boysie Oakes as he fell heavily to the floor.

He was still on the floor a few moments later when consciousness began to return. A lot of people seemed to be talking at once, and he could distinguish two faces peering down at him. One was male, and obviously official. The other female and as palatable as they come—dark almond eyes set beautifully against a smooth complexion. A wide trembling mouth, and a soft fall of tawny hair. Even in this twilit state, Boysie could appreciate the glitter of concern in her eyes.

The mist began to clear. The official gentleman, who was actually an assistant manager, clucked over him like a hen about to discharge an ostrich-size, quadruple-yolked egg:

"Mr Oakes? You OK, Mr Oakes? That this should have happened here. A terrible thing. Truly terrible thing. Now are you OK, Mr Oakes?"

"Receiving you strength two. No, I am not OK," said Boysie, his eyes taking great bites out of the female who was now regarding him not only with concern but also with blatant sensual fascination. Together, the floor manager and the girl helped Boysie to his feet. The room did a stall turn, then began to fall into a spin. Boysie sat down on the bed, and with the fingertips of his right hand, gently felt the tender spot below his left ear. To the touch it was as though something large, round, and bristling with poisoned darts, had got under his skin.

"Think we ought to call a doctor, Mr Oakes? We've got a physician right here in the hotel. You're goin' to have a nasty bruise there."

"Be all right." Boysie tried to do a tough, gritted-teeth smile; but even that hurt, so he did a brave wince instead.

"Er, I haven't notified the police or anything yet, Mr Oakes, I mean. Well, I was wondering. The publicity. The hotel. It's my job to see the guests are comfortable and that the hotel is protected. You. You wouldn't sue the hotel, would you, Mr Oakes? You a Government guest and all. It's terrible. New York, we get robberies and beatings, muggings all the time. Central Park you dare not go into alone at night, especially if you happen to be a lady." The assistant manager looked at the tawny-haired wonder, pleading for confirmation. Boysie, beginning to feel a little better, could see the man was desperately

46

embarrassed. An assault actually in the hotel could, he imagined, dent its reputation and buckle trade into an economic concertina. Very early in his professional life Boysie had learned that it was better to keep the police and other public bodies right out of the picture.

"Don't worry about it. Accident. Think no more about it —Ow!" He groaned as the swelling began to pulse out a fresh series of pain jerks.

"It's really lucky your friend turned up."

Boysie looked round for his friend, then realised that the hotel type meant the beauty who had, by this time, joined him on the edge of the bed. So far she had not said a word. Now she spoke, and, to Boysie, the whole string section of the New York Philharmonic seemed to come drifting into the room.

"Poor baby," she put a protective arm on Boysie's shoulder. "Lucky I turned up, wasn't it, honey?"

"Well, if you're sure it's OK. I'll send up an ice pack for that bruise." The official was hovering.

"I'll look after him now." Coming from those succulent lips, the phrase was one of distinct promise.

"I'll drop by later. Just to see if you need anything. OK, Mr Oakes?"

Boysie, now almost himself, except for the pounding of a miniature pneumatic drill down the left side of his face, was about to tell the man not to bother, when the soft hunk of womanhood by his side cut in with:

"How kind of you, but please don't worry. Mr Oakes'll call down if he wants anything."

The floor manager backed out of the room muttering soothing noises: "Anything the hotel can do. Last thing we would have had happen. Given us all quite a shock. And the Vassar Alumanae dinner coming up and all . . ." The door shut out the man's burblings and Boysie was left alone with his head, and the slim assembly of curves.

"Hallo," said the girl.

"Hallo," said Boysie. They looked at each other in candid appreciation.

"You're Boysie Oakes," she said, moving a little closer.

"Yes, I know. Who are you?"

"Max sent me. Didn't he tell you? We're going to sunny California."

Boysie grinned with pleasure.

"Someone did call to say my travelling companion would be over. But I didn't really expect . . . Well . . . I . . ." He paused. Somewhere in the rear of his mind there was a picture of himself doing obeisance to Mostyn: offering a garland of thanks for the goodies that were coming his way. For this, it was worth being physically assaulted.

"Do you have a name, or a number, or do people just say 'Wow', or 'Cor' or something?" he asked, trying to forget the headache—a reasonably easy operation when the other parts of the body began taking one's mind off the pain.

"I'm Chicory." She sounded like someone announcing the result of a charade.

"Chicory," repeated Boysie.

"Chicory Triplehouse."

"Triplehouse."

"Yep. And don't ask me where I got it. We didn't come over with the Pilgrim Fathers. We weren't pioneers of the old West. We aren't an established Southern family, and none of my relatives are members of the Ivy League—yet with a name like Triplehouse they ought to be. I guess the Triplehouses just happened."

"Where did you happen?"

"Joplin, Missouri—which is about as hick as you can get. No, our family tree seems to have withered just before my grandmammy and grandpappy were granted the faculty of memory. Someone turned over a stone and there they were—Triplehouses—equipped with a certain resilience and a warped sense of humour."

Boysie offered her a Chesterfield and lit the cigarettes. She smoked like a man, he noticed, holding the white tube confidently and close to her lips, taking draughts of smoke right down into the lungs and expelling them in a thin stream with her mouth in a whistling attitude.

"Just to show you," she continued. "My grandpappy had my daddy baptised Stephen Howard Ian. Stephen Howard Ian Triplehouse. Can you imagine? Never dared sign his initials, let alone have them engraved in gold on his briefcase or whatever."

Boysie gurgled, and a knock at the door announced the presence of a white-coated serf bearing an ice pack.

"How about those two characters?" said Chicory when the servant had disappeared leaving Boysie clasping the ice to his lump. "They ran like blue hell when I screamed. What were they after?"

"Haven't the foggiest."

"New York can be a bit like that, but it doesn't usually happen in hotels—except to film stars and all, with lots of loot. Or for publicity. Couldn't be anything to do with your work, could it?"

Boysie felt the whirlpool of anxiety begin to spin in his stomach. The lushness of Chicory Triplehouse had acted as a soporific, now he began to think more clearly about the brace of horror comics, their insistence that he should come with them to Siedler, his refusal, and the ultimate violence. Undoubtedly it was something to do with his work. The trip to San Diego, the lying in the sun, the starlets done to a turn on the beaches, the one solitary day to be spent watching a missile being fired: it had all sounded too easy. There had to be a catch somewhere. The palpitating, red prominence behind his ear was tangible proof of the catch.

"Well, could it?" Chicory was looking at him, a tiny knot of worry marring the smooth area between her long pencilled eyebrows.

"I suppose it might be." Boysie felt his guts flap violently. "Think I'd better try and make it to the bathroom." He hobbled over to the door. The floor swayed slightly for the first few steps, then became stable and firm.

When he returned, Chicory was talking, *sotto voce*, into the telephone: "Yes, Max, sure baby, but do you think it's really necessary? What gives anyway? Sure he's a dreamboat but what is he, like some crazy diplomat, royalty or something? OK if you say so. Sure, he's just come back. He's here now. You want to talk to him? OK, honey, and you." To Boysie: "Boysie honey, Max wants to talk to you."

Boysie took the telephone from the cool hand. She moved away, allowing her fingers to brush lightly along the back of his arm. He could just feel the nails vaguely scratching through his shirt; giving him a shudder of pleasure.

" 'L?' " He remembered the voice at the other end of the line.

"Yes."

"*USS One.*"

"Yes?" Boysie made a mental note to find out who the blazes *USS One* was. Might be the President for all he knew.

"Chicky tells me there's been trouble."

"A little." Boysie's natural pride flared for a second. "We handled it," he said casually.

"The way I heard it you would have been clobbered good and proper if Chicky hadn't turned up and done her celebrated impression of a screech-owl. This is a little disturbing, you know. Was it the opposition?"

"Well, it could have been."

A silence. Then: "All right, we'll just make a slight change in plan. In case they're on to something. But I can't honestly see what it has to do with the present operation. More likely it's an organisation out to get you for your past affiliations. The old liquidation bit. You never had to bump a member of the Mafia, did you?"

The whirlpool's vortex increased its power, now situated somewhere just below the bile duct. Boysie could have screamed. Did that smooth bastard Mostyn tell everyone? Was he ever going to get away from the time when officially he was the Liquidator, the private executioner, for the Department of Special Security?

"I suppose it could be the past," he said weakly.

"All right. We were going to fly you out. But I've told Chicky that we'll fix alternative transport—for part of the way at least. If they are after you they'll have a pretty good watch on the airfields and railroad depots. I think you'd better call your contact with the locals. See what he says about the situation. Chicky will give you the rest of the dope. You're OK, aren't you, 'L'? No bones broken or anything?"

Boysie was beginning to take the first steps into gloom. "I'm all right," he said, sounding as disinterested as he felt. He replaced the receiver.

"Hey, now what are you looking so miserable about, Boysie baby?" Chicory was back on the corner of the bed, her head cocked on one side, a seductive mouth lifted in an inviting smile. Boysie looked at her with relish. Ungentlemanly relish. She was wearing a navy crêpe suit with bold chalk stripes slashing down the material, and had thrown off her jacket, revealing—to very full effect—the white blouse with a centrally embroidered sunburst design. Her legs were crossed, and the slim skirt affectionately hugged her thigh, then slid smoothly down the leg, ending in two sunny inches of nylon above the knee. She was the most delightful thing on which Boysie had set his lustful eyes. Since Priscilla Braddock-Fairchild, anyway.

"Well . . ." For a moment Boysie looked like a recalcitrant schoolboy. "Your mate, Max, says there are some changes in our schedule."

"Schedule, skedule, schmedule." The sunburst design wiggled as she inhaled. "And it's me that should be miserable. We're doin' the journey by bus. Some of it anyhow. By bus?" She made a disgusted, clucking noise, rolling her eyes upwards. "Max thinks it'll be safer to mingle with the herd. We leave on the noon hour, he's sending the tickets over, and they're goin' to let us know where we can change to a nice cool jet. But it's about three days West—some horrible hot dump like Oklahoma City or Albuquerque." She gave a heavy mock sigh. "It's goin' ta be a long ride, boy, so pack yo deodorant, yo sure need it on them thar buses." Chicory threw back her head and laughed. "Now come on, take me out to dinner and I'll show you the sights."

"I've got to call someone first," said Boysie, remembering Siedler and rooting in the bedside drawer for the envelope

51

with the two telephone numbers. "And I don't know whether I really should go out."

"Why the heck not?"

"Those two characters . . ."

"If they're still waiting for you, you'll be a darned sight safer out in a crowd than sitting up here alone."

"I wasn't thinking about being alone," said Boysie, finding the envelope. "I was considering a nice quiet dinner for two. Up here. You know, the soft lights and sweet music thing."

Chicory smiled—warm and comfortable: "Nothing I'd like better, honey, but I have a rule. Stupid, but it's the only one I've ever made and the only one I've ever managed to keep in the whole of my long low adult life."

"Oh? Rules are made to be broken. What is it anyway?"

"Simple. I don't—on first dates. And really, Boysie, this is a first date. You're cute, I like you a lot, and you and I both know darned well what's going to happen if we have dinner up here. Sure, it'll happen anyway—maybe in Oklahoma City, maybe out in San Diego. It'll happen, we both knew that soon as we saw one another. Chemistry. But I'm not going to break my little old rule; and you don't want to spoil my record, do you, hon?" She got up and moved over to him.

Before he had time to answer, Chicory had coiled her arms round his neck and their lips were tethered together—open wide, fluttering, sucking the breath from each other's lungs while their tongues spliced in intricate patterns between their teeth. At last she pushed him gently away.

"You make your call, Boysie honey." She was speaking softly, scant-breathed. "The sooner we're out of here, the more sure I am of not breaking my rule." At the bathroom door, she murmured: "Sometime soon, Boysie. That's for sure. Sometime very soon."

It took five minutes to locate Joe Siedler who was full of apologies after Boysie told his story.

"Boysie pal, we wouldn't have had this happen for anything. But I guess your man was right—something hanging over from the past. I'm goin' to make sure though. I'm going to make cer-

tain that you stay in one piece. You wanna go out? Sure. I'll
have one a the boys look after you, at a distance of course. Now
don't you worry 'bout a thing Boysie buddy, we'll take good
care of you, and I'll be over personally, but personally, first
thing in the morning just to make sure you get outa town with
no bother. OK? Now you have yourself a real swell time. And
don't worry, we'll be watching out for you. Real good."

Boysie and Chicory dined in the Rainbow Room of the RCA
Building: in a restaurant which looked as unreal as a movie set.
Even the air seemed to have been impregnated with luxury—
sprayed from hygienic cans. They sat at a table window, from
which they could see out over Manhattan to the Hudson—a
great fairyland of tiny lights and flickering neon; a huge, rising
castellation pricked through with bright oblongs, twinkling in
lines up to the sky; bulwarks of midnight-blue against the deep
pearl of the night.

With Lobster Remoulade, Roast Long Island Duckling, and
a splendid Strawberry Shortcake inside them, they took the
chrome-lined elevator back to earth (Boysie had been frightened
enough going up. Going down—with the drop of about fifty
storeys before the brakes came on—was purgatory. But Chicory
revelled in the whole business). For two hours they wandered
through the streets of New York—Times Square, with its
brash glare, noise, music and huckster atmosphere—the huge
Camel ad puffing smoke from the painted cardboard man's
gaping mouth; then along the Great White Way, where the
Broadway babies don't say goodnight until it's early morning.

The streets began to empty—sad wisps of steam, rising from
the covers of the city's piped heating system, wavering as a
yellow cab growled past or a prowl car hovered along the kerb.
On Fifth Avenue, with their reflections dancing in the high
mirrors of plate glass, they touched hands and held on tight,
walking inches from the spangled jewels and chic dresses safe
in the display windows: silent, lonely, unwanted until the regi-
ments took to the streets and offices and department stores and
the city came alive again.

They said goodnight and kissed outside the plushiest store,

Saks, on the corner of Fifth Avenue and 50th Street. Boysie felt like a seventeen-year-old. But, to be fair, that was how he always felt when a new and sensual female clawed her way into his easy heart. At a few yards distance—across the road, on the steps of St Patrick's Cathedral—a United States Internal Security officer called Bremoy, who had the worried look of a man on the verge of his first ulcer, watched the kiss and, under his breath, snarled something about "Bastard top agents and their whores."

Bremoy was unaware that he too was being observed. In the shadow of the fifteen-foot bronze Atlas which decorates the forecourt of the International Building, across the intersection from St Patrick's, a young man stood biting his nails—his eyes darting between Bremoy and the osculating couple. The skin on the young man's face was taut to the bone. It was a face like a skull.

HAVING FIRST looked, with routine care, under the bed, in the bathroom, behind the shower curtain and in the wardrobe, Boysie locked the door. Stripping off his jacket and shirt, he ambled back to the bathroom, popped the plug into place and began to run warm water into the tub. "Love is a Many Splendoured Thing," sang Boysie in a quavering and fraction off-key tenor. Returning to the bedroom he undressed to his jockey briefs, and was about to make the journey back to the bathroom, when a thought slid slyly into his mind. Picking up his discarded trousers he fumbled for the small set of keys left carelessly in a pocket. Finding them, he pulled the tan Revelation from the wardrobe, unlocked it and unzipped the special compartment built into the lid. Slipping his hand into the cavity, Boysie pulled out the small pearl-handled automatic pistol and checked its mechanism. It was a pistol which could in no circumstances be regarded as heavy artillery—a Saur & Sohn Type 1A adapted for .22 ammunition—but it always gave him that smug feeling of satisfaction; an added sense of superiority and power. He carried it quite illegally; and, while Mostyn would have had a dozen fits—in variegated colours—

had he known that Boysie even possessed such a weapon, its psychological value paid off dividends of colossal proportions. The pistol was loaded. The safety catch on. Boysie smiled and carried the gun into the bathroom. He would keep it handy, he resolved, for the rest of this American jaunt.

CIRIO WAS tall with full undulating grey hair which seemed to set a standard colour to his personality. By birth he was Italian, though it was many years since he had seen the terraced vineyards around his family's home near Castel San Pietro. By trade he was a restaurateur: owner and manager of the *Club Fondante*—a medium-class nightspot in the East 70s. By profession, Cirio was a Communist.

Cirio sat at his desk in the back room office at the *Club Fondante*, the long square-tipped nails of his right-hand fingers drumming an agitated tattoo on the stained woodwork. To his left, the strong-arm boys who had called on Boysie earlier that evening were seated side by side. The one with the scar below his eye was quietly picking his teeth with his free hand—the right arm hung interestingly in a sling; the other merely looked into space, as though locked in some private, and ghoulish, nightmare.

Across the desk from Cirio, a man in his late thirties was engrossed in lighting a cigar. He was a person who radiated authority—expensive authority, and, as he drew on his cigar, he looked up at Cirio with steel-grey eyes which cut into the Italian like an oxyacetylene lamp burning into soft metal.

"You are a lot of goddam prissy bastards," announced the steel-eyed man with feeling.

"Look, Ritzy, the boys did their best. We're sorry, but it just couldn't be helped."

"Damn broad turned up and started screaming her lousy little head off," muttered the hood with the scar.

"Their best ain't enough. They gotta do better than their best." Ritzy spoke with the chill of a deep freeze—outside, at the North Pole. "Now, I suppose, you bums expect me to get ya out of the mess."

55

Cirio did not answer. Ritzy spoke again: "Look, howdya think I feel? This organisation is expected ta carry out assault operations. That's its function—its purpose. We're all paid good money—good American dollars—because we're supposed to be professional men. We're supposed to be proficient. Get me? Ya do know what proficient means?" Once more nobody spoke. "I got six assault groups working under me in this city alone. And I choose you boys 'cause I reckon you're the best in the business. What are the contractors goin' ta say ta me when they find that we loused up the deal? Waddam I goin' to say to them? Goddam it, Cirio . . ."

The telephone burred out its alarm. Cirio spoke into the mouthpiece:

"Yea? . . . He is? . . . OK, just stay there and watch . . . Good boy, you're doin' a swell job."

Ritzy looked questioningly.

"Young Skull Face," said Cirio. "The subject's returned to his hotel. Said goodnight to the broad outside Saks. Necking like crazy the kid says."

"Sexy bastards, the English!" spat Ritzy. "OK. We can't get him outa there. So he's gotta be eliminated. So there'll have ta be an accident. I wanted t'avoid it but . . . Gimme that phone." He thought for a moment, then began to stab at the dial. They could hear the signal burping at the other end, then a voice answered. Ritzy leaned back in his chair: "That you, Dim? . . . Ritzy . . . How ya bin? . . . Look, Dim, ya remember ya fixed me up with a little pet way back, when was it? Oh, couple of years back . . . Yea, that's it, boy, you remember good . . . You got another of them things? . . . Huhn hu . . . Huhn hu . . . Yea, that's it. OK, I'll collect it personally my-self . . . And Dim, I'll need your help tucking it away. Same like last time." He laughed and, after an exchange of what passed among Ritzy's friends for courtesies, put the phone down and turned back to Cirio. "Now, you're goin' ta learn some-thing. I'm goin' ta show youse guys a real professional job. A real live circus act. And our friend in the New Weston Hotel just ain't goin' ta know what hit him. You got the list of the

56

guy's closest friends comin' out on the boat?" Cirio nodded. "Yea, there was one in particular," continued Ritzy. "Babe with a fancy English name . . ."

Once more they were interrupted by the telephone. "OK, bring him right up," said Cirio, after listening to the brief message. Then, looking at Ritzy: "He's arrived."

When the visitor was shown into the room, the two hoodlums stopped picking and staring. Their mouths dropped open.

"But, that's the guy . . ." said one.

"That's him. The guy we was supposed ta . . ."

"Come in, friend. Welcome to the United States." Ritzy and Cirio had risen to their feet. "No, gentlemen," said Ritzy. "This is not the guy. This one is . . . Well, like a duplicate: a twin soul."

Vladimir Solev, tired and a mite nervous, smiled, at his new companions. The left side of his mouth turned up more sharply than ever. The likeness to Boysie Oakes was staggering.

III – ...AND LEAVE THE DRIVING TO US

THE door of the bus slid open. The driver was smiling down at a young couple waiting to greet their aunt, or mother, or whoever she was. The elderly lady appeared in the doorway, looking fresh and neat. A porter—flashing a twenty-five-cent beam—stepped forward to help her down. The young couple embraced the lady, who seemed to be the incarnation of all nice American aunts and mothers, commenting on how well and refreshed she looked.

"Oh, but it's great travelling Greyhound!" enthused the elderly lady.

A quartet of songsters started up the jingle: "Go *Greyhound* ... And leave the driving to us." The television screen cut to the next commercial.

"And that's how we go, Boysie honey," purred Chicory, sitting curled in an armchair, clasping her glass of Old Hickory to her glorious left breast. "They say the first hundred miles are the worst. No, it'll be great. With you it'll be great."

Boysie folded a pair of denim beach slacks, and placed them tenderly on top of the clothes already stacked into the Revelation. That completed his packing. He turned and gave the girl a long, sizzling look. Chicory was all set for the journey, claret skin-tight stretch pants and a plain white light sweater appeared to be the only clothes she was wearing. At any rate, one could detect no ridge or bump of undergarments. Pondering on the possibility of there being none at all, Boysie strolled into the bathroom and went through his routine check of the automatic pistol—his third since the affair with the two heavies on the previous evening—slipping it back into the patent holster stitched inside the hip pocket of his charcoal casual slacks.

It was exactly ten-thirty when he returned to the bedroom to snap the Revelation shut. They had an hour and a half to go before the bus was due to leave the Port Authority Bus Terminal to carry them West over the slaving miles of hot road. Boysie swallowed the last of his drink and decided that now was the time to put in a little more work on softening up the ornamental Miss Triplehouse. Since her arrival—on the pre-arranged dot of ten—he had noticed, with pleasure, the warmth of her look—her eyes following him around the room as he packed his suitcase; that longing gaze of adoration which so flatters men, and is one of woman's most cunning ruses in the game of seduction. Now, he moved towards her, settling on the corner of the armchair, one hand sliding across her back to knead her left shoulder. Chicory lifted her face, closed her eyes, and allowed her mouth to open slightly, ready to receive his. Boysie bent closer: "It's our second date, isn't it, lovey?" His voice trembling on the edge of excitement.

"Yes," she whispered.

"And we've got all of an hour before we need leave."

"Huhn-hu?"

Their lips touched, and Joe Siedler started a friendly tattoo on the door. "Blast," emoted Boysie, who had forgotten Siedler's promise to come over and see them safely off the premises.

Sielder was as boisterous as ever, and genuinely appreciative when he set eyes on Chicory. "Geez, you British sure know how to pick 'em," he gushed. "Wish I were riding down to San Diego with a honey like you, honey. Hey, Boysie pal, while you're down there, do me a favour, look up the head bartender at the *Bali Hai*. Name o' Bruno. A real nut. But real. Old Buddy o' mine."

Joe in his fulsome way was determined to see that Boysie's last hours in New York were pleasant, and that the couple were moved on and out of his territory without any difficulties.

"I got Avallon and the automobile downstairs waitin' for youse. And a couple of the boys are outside in the lobby justa make sure," he said, smiling proudly at this display of efficiency.

"Yes, I saw them on my way in," said Chicory. "Got Cop stamped all over them in red ink, and two darned great bulges in their jackets. Worried me."

"Aw, hell! It shows, doesn't it? I keep telling the Organisation they want people like me. Inconspicuous people." Siedler in his wild check jacket was about as inconspicuous as a harlot at a harvest festival.

"It's the same with our police," said Boysie dryly. "Damn great boots, and they all wear the same kind of raincoat."

A puzzled look crept over Chicory's face: "Boysie? Why are the cops playing guardian angel to you?" There was an embarrassed pause.

"Oh well, you know . . . When you're negotiating a big government contract . . . and after that silly spot of bother last night." Boysie tailed off lamely. The pause continued for the count of ten.

"How about a little drink before I put you on that bus," said Siedler, realising that he had made some kind of a boo-boo, changing the subject rapidly, and producing another bottle of Old Hickory which he had been clutching ostentatiously behind his back. "How about that? Hickory for Chicory." He caught sight of the TV screen. "And man do I go for Yogi Bear. Just look at that." Siedler went off into gusts of mirth as the popular bear once more outwitted the ranger at Jellystone Park. He stood for a full minute, oblivious to everything else, transfixed by the antics of the cartoon characters. Boysie finally detached the bottle from a limp hand and carted it over to the dressing table.

He was about to pour the drinks when a bell boy arrived bearing an unexpected gift. The parcel was for Boysie—large, oblong, flat and beautifully packaged.

"Christmas already?" said Siedler as Boysie placed the interesting object on the table.

"Who the hell's sending parcels to me here?" Boysie felt an initial intuitive nip of danger. Siedler was behind him.

"Wait a minute, boy. Careful with that thing. You can never tell—specially if someone's gunning for you. Better let me get it down to headquarters. You know, after last night's caper. They'll get the Bomb Squad on to it."

"There's a card on top," said the observant Chicory.

Boysie removed the envelope from beneath its cellotape binding, slit it open and took out a square, gilt-edged card. The writing was in that round, characterless hand much favoured by the upper-bracket girls' schools along the Roedean and Cheltenham circuit.

Got your address from the Cunard people, it read. *Hope this reaches you before you leave New York. A little gift for making me so happy. With my love ever. Priscilla.*

"Gosh," burbled Boysie. "How jolly nice of her. Wonder what she's sent?"

"Who's Priscilla?" said Chicory in a voice betraying the green-eyed monster which lurks in the hot recesses of every woman's brain.

"Oh, just a girl I met on the boat. Nobody important." Boysie threw it off with an inexpert touch of nonchalance.

"Hu!" She tossed her head and went over to study the view from the window as Boysie scrabbled with the outer wrapping.

"You're sure it's OK?" asked Siedler, facing Boysie over the parcel.

"This is all right. Girl on the boat. Hundred per center. Jolly nice of her to have bothered." Boysie preened like a birthday boy. The wrapping was off now, revealing an elegant long box, crested with the name of one of New York's swankiest stores for men. He struggled to remove the lid—fingers all thumbs.

"Here, let me help you with that." Siedler pulled up on his side of the box, disclosing a first layer of tissue paper.

Boysie and Siedler must have both realised the dreadful mistake at the same moment—just as the lid came free. Joe Siedler's hand was outstretched over the tissue. He stood no chance. The tissue stirred and crackled, then seemed to burst upwards like an opening flower. The long, thin body flashed out from its paper retreat and streaked with lightning speed and grace, fastening its dripping little mouth hard on to Siedler's wrist. He gave a shriek of terror. Boysie took a half step back then stopped, fascinated, screwed to the floor, hands paralysed with horror. Chicory turned and began to scream, a forearm thrown across her face as though in defence. The revolting, deadly fangs of the eight-foot black mamba had closed tightly and were relentlessly pumping venom into Siedler's bloodstream. For a moment he did not move, his eyes dilated, all senses fixed on the hot pulse of pain and awful crawling sensation. Then, with an almost listless downward jerk of the arm, Siedler shook the brute free and fell back on the bed, moaning and clutching his arm. The snake flicked its soft green-black body —sending the box flying—rolled on to the floor with a slithery thump, then seemed to leap forward, its length whipping out so that the tail almost touched Chicory's feet by the window. The snake's tiny eyes gleamed above the darting tongue. For a second it seemed to be making up its mind which way to turn; then, head slightly raised, it made an effortless rise on to the bed and began to glide like an arrow towards Boysie.

The mamba is one of the world's most dangerous and aggressive snakes. It is also one of the fastest. In Africa they tell stories about good runners being overtaken by a mamba on the hunt. Boysie felt the hair on his neck stand erect. But the nervous, inbred instinct for self-preservation, and those few seconds which Siedler had taken to throw the snake from his wrist, gave Boysie just enough time to go through a standard reaction. The little pearl-handled pistol was out. He experienced that terrifying flip-roll of his stomach and saw the blurred head of the nauseating creature speeding over the bed coming straight for him.

His third shot caught the snake in the head—the other two went thudding into the bed, close to where Siedler lay moaning. A fourth bullet entered the middle of the reptile's pliable body. It reared up, then dropped writhing and lashing in a death fury to the floor. Boysie, trembling with terror, hung on to the table. Chicory was screaming. At that moment the door crashed open and the two policemen slammed into the room, their M1911/A automatics at the ready.

THE GROANING had stopped, and Chicory's hysteria was now reduced to a whisper. One of the men was talking urgently into the telephone. The other, who had been applying a makeshift tourniquet to Siedler's arm, suddenly raised himself from the stooping position over the bed. A choking sound came from Siedler's throat. Boysie saw him twitch twice, and watched the white bubble of foam come slavering from his lips. Siedler took two great gulps of air, then seemed to deflate, his head falling loosely on to the pillow.

"Joe's not goin' to need the antivenom, nor a doctor," said the cop to his colleague. "Musta been the shock, or his heart. Poison wouldn't have worked that quick."

The other man went on talking into the telephone. Boysie looked down at the still, ashen figure of Joe Siedler. He felt numb and his bowels had turned watery. Through the confused and shocked thoughts, jumbled in his mind, Boysie reflected that he was a natural Jonah: a magnet for violence: a carrier of death. This kind of thing had happened before. He remembered a villa in Southern France, and a young girl's body spurting its lifeblood over the bonnet of a car, and the corpses of nearly thirty people whose deaths he had caused— one way or another—since the day when smooth Mostyn had offered him a post with the Department of British Special Security. Now, the gay, friendly Joe Siedler, whom he had met only a few hours before, lay dead; two tiny swelling punctures in his wrist.

"He's not . . .?" Chicory looked up, her dark eyes ringed with the puff of tears.

Boysie nodded and went over to her. She clutched his hand, her fingers moving against his in the nervous caress of fear.

"Who are you?" she asked, frightened and low.

"Boysie Oakes," he whispered. "A bloody leper."

"OK, there ain't much more you can do here." The policeman had put down the telephone. "We've gotta get you on your way, fast as we can. The lady would like to freshen up a bit first?"

Chicory nodded and went slowly, trembling, to the bathroom.

"Joe was a great guy," said the other cop.

"A great-hearted guy," said his colleague. "Mr Oakes, I guess we ought to get a few details straightened out."

Boysie answered their questions about the arrival of the parcel, the character and connections of Miss Priscilla Braddock-Fairchild, and the actual events which had filled the room with half a minute of terror. Together, they examined the box in which the horrific gift had arrived. It was lined with a kind of protective foil—which retained unpleasant traces of the former occupant. The reptile had been coiled securely, obviously by an expert, between a series of forked prongs set in a spiral at the bottom of the box. The lid contained similar prongs. The snake—which they had pushed carefully into a corner and covered with a sheet—had, presumably, been drugged and fitted snugly into its lair, where it had lain, immobile, until the dope had worn off and the lid was lifted to free it to the attack.

"Nice-minded sort of character who thought this one up," said the cop as Chicory rejoined them. "OK, Mr Oakes? Miss Triplehouse?" He looked briskly at his watch. "Time to get moving. Joe's office say they'll be keeping an eye on you, and that you'll be moved off the bus at the first opportunity. We got some of their boys coming over to square the hotel and get things done nice for Joe."

"He was a great guy," mused the other man. "A regular guy."

They took Boysie and Chicory out of the hotel, by a back exit, to a stunned and silent Avallon who drove them through the hot blaring streets to the crowded Port Authority Bus Terminal. The big, air-conditioned Sceni-cruiser growled out into Dyer Avenue, bound for Los Angeles, dead on noon.

"Ya change buses at Flagstaff, Arizona—that'll be day after tomorrow," the driver had said examining their tickets.

Boysie and Chicory, leaning back in their comfortable air-line-type seats, held hands and wordlessly tried to wipe from their minds the picture of Joe Siedler's face contorted by fear and anguish as the great slim snake clung to his arm. As the bus turned down the ramp into the Lincoln Tunnel, heading towards the Pennsylvania Turnpike, the full dimensions of what had happened suddenly rammed home into Boysie's whirling mind. He felt unclean, as he always did when death moved near to him. The black mamba had been meant for him. By rights it should be him, and not Joe Siedler, lying in a mortuary, cold and rigid as frozen meat. For once he seemed to be facing the situation with relative calm. Shock had pushed out panic. But those clear blue eyes gleamed hard and the left corner of his mouth jerked up in the reflex which was almost his trademark. Both were signs of the ingrained fear, which Boysie Oakes had to fight nearly every day of his life.

At the same moment, the skull-faced youth was standing in a telephone booth in the big, glistening babel that is the New York Port Authority Bus Terminal.

"Yea, kid, we just heard," said Cirio at the other end of the line. "Thanks, kid. You'd better come on over here. We all got work to do."

In his office at the *Club Fondante* Cirio put down the telephone and gazed across the desk at a disconsolate Ritzy. "You're the boss," he said—sort of snide.

"Yea. I'd better call head office," said Ritzy.

MOSTYN WAS just about to leave the headquarters building off Whitehall when his secretary brought in the decoded cable from *USS One*: the Department's undercover man in New York. Mostyn was a very worried man. The signal, now on the desk in front of him read:

ONE ATTEMPT TO ABDUCT ONE TO LIQUIDATE 'L' YOUR DEPUTY OBSERVER PLAYBOY AND TREPHOLITE TRIALS STOP CIA ESCORT KILLED STOP 'L' AND OUR FEMALE ESCORT NOW EN ROUTE STOP ADVISE STOP

Mostyn felt lonely. His intuition had been right again. The final word, 'ADVISE' winked at him hysterically from the paper. The ball had been pitched firmly into his court. Somehow Boysie was in it again. Right up to his neck. "Hope to God he's got his brown suit on," muttered Mostyn as he picked up the direct line telephone to the Chief.

The Chief had already left. Mostyn got through to the Duty Officer. "Number Two here." He spoke rapidly, his senses alert to the urgency which, presumably, lay behind the cable. "Get me the Chief. Top Priority."

IN THE middle of the afternoon they stopped, along the Turnpike, at the Howard Johnson restaurant near Mechanicsville—a regulation building of clean stone with a slate roof. It reminded Boysie a little of the quiet afternoon he had spent in the Cotswolds on his last leave. Elizabeth, the girl who had been with him then, was very different from Chicory, and his world far more peaceful. They ate Mr Johnson's celebrated Southern Fried Chicken (which tastes not unlike his American Baked Ham—so fine is the art of cutting the highs and lows off the taste spectrum) and French Fries, washing the meal down with scalding coffee. The whole business took only twenty indigestible minutes. Then, rest stop over, the bus grumbled its way out on to the ribbon of tarmac once more.

Night closed in and the bus ploughed into the neon jungle of advertising which is the unnatural scenery of the Eastern States: Piggly-Wiggly Stores, Go TWA, Shop at Schneiders, El Rancho, Bar-B-Q, He'll be Safe With Jukey's—Best Morticians in Town. Indianapolis went by unnoticed in the early hours, and when they woke the view was of the long tobacco fields, elegant clapboard houses and high barns of Indiana.

Throughout the day they chatted in fragments, Boysie shifting the conversation over to Chicory's past whenever the talk came dangerously near to his own. By the time they reached Springfield, Missouri, he had heard about her childhood in Joplin (Springfield made her nostalgic), home-made cookies, wire teeth braces, pigtails (all part of the great American saga, thought Boysie: Andy Hardy and all that jazz). After Spring-field there were the more interesting, and undoubtedly more glamorous, tales of New York and the model racket; then the wealthy husband who, after a two-year idyll with Chicory, had walked off with a counter assistant from Woolworths, called Ophelia Cocks. Thus Chicory reverted to her maiden name of Triplehouse and accepted the wayward husband's sizeable alimony.

"Now," she said with a pout, mimicking a hick accent, "I'm nuthin' more'n a bored pussy, holdin' off the tom cats and keepin' out of the kitten way."

Night again, and the conversation petered out in fitful sleep. Boysie's mind clicked back to New York: the abortive attempt to entice him from the hotel, and the subtle horror of the mamba. Try as he would, the pictures kept returning, shoul-dering their way into his dozing thoughts. The conclusion was always the same. Behind this seemingly simple operation, there lurked that old last enemy, death. Twice in New York. They would not let it go at that. There was purpose and method be-hind the two attempts. Sometime, soon, they would have an-other go. Boysie swallowed, and allowed his hand to stray to the satisfyingly hard butt of the pistol in his hip pocket. Third time lucky? It was all Mostyn's fault. It was always Mostyn's fault. Boysie began his favourite pastime of silently cursing his Second-in-Command.

They slept a little and woke in Tulsa ("This is the place that chap was twenty-four hours from," said Boysie. Chicory giggled), again in Oklahoma City, and once more in Amarillo, Texas, where the crickets were singing fit to snap their tiny wings. Sleep again, a little deeper, and at six in the morning, with the sun rising over the spectacular desert, the Scenicruiser pulled up in front of the Posting House Cafe, Santa Rosa, New Mexico.

"You gotta nour here, folks," said the driver.

Yawning and stretching, the bleary passengers lurched stiffly towards their respective rest rooms—cutely labelled "Señors" and "Señoritas"—and allowed the gastric juices to flow unimpeded at the thought of breakfast served by raven-sleek Spanish-American beauties who could be glimpsed behind the restaurant counters.

The water was cold, the other male passengers bawdy and loud. It reminded Boysie of army days; freezing in the ablutions surrounded by false heartiness. He never could shave with cold water, and performed the operation painfully, cutting himself twice and drying the blood with little pieces of toilet paper. His tingling Onyx after-shave lotion stung more than usual; there was a very rude drawing, accompanied by an Anglo-Saxon word, etched on the lavatory wall. "Just like home," murmured Boysie, realising that his travelling companions had all shaved, shined their shoes, and done the other thing at the double. They were now probably wolfing all the remaining hotcakes, crispy cereals, bacon, sunnyside-up eggs and coffee. He packed his shaving gear back into the neat green Lentheric Onyx de Luxe travel kit and—after taking one last look at his parting in the cracked mirror—turned towards the door.

"Mr Oakes?" The man spoke conspiratorially, leaning against the wall outside the rest room. He looked nattily expensive, his chin barbered as though someone had plucked out each hair independently by the roots and then given the skin a going over with varnish. Boysie stared into a pair of eyes which commanded attention. At first sight this was not the kind of man with whom Boysie felt an instinctive kinship.

"Yes?" Boysie's hand prepared to move towards his hip pocket. The man's right hand came forward and flipped open a leather identity wallet. Boysie caught sight of a badge and official-looking card.

"Henniger," said Henniger. "United States Security. Have your breakfast with the girl, collect your baggage from the bus, and meet us at the car out in back. Red Mustang convertible."

"Thank God for that," said Chicory, her mouth full of hotcake and syrup, when Boysie told her. "I've just about had that bus. Or I should say it's just about had me. Those seats on your tail! Yow!"

The car was parked at the rear of the Cafe—the sun, already climbing with all systems 'Go' on a smooth trajectory, reflecting in a bonnet which looked hygenically clean. Henniger made no move to help Boysie as he humped his Revelation, and Chicory's lightweight case, over the few yards of parking lot. Behind the wheel sat a tall lean man with grey well-toned hair and glasses.

"This is Mr Henniger," said Boysie affably as they reached the car. Chicory smiled. "Miss Triplehouse."

"Howdy, Miss Triplehouse; you and Mr Oakes in back, please."

"Gee, are we glad to see you," said Chicory, ducking her head and sliding delicately into the rear seat. "We thought we'd be on that bus till ever." Boysie stood, looking lost, with the cases.

"Better put those in the trunk, hadn't you, Mr Oakes?" smiled Henniger, still making no move to help him. "It's unlocked."

With the luggage stowed away and Boysie snug beside Chicory, the car boomed out on to the road and began to eat up the miles which lash out painfully between the vast stretch of scrubby New Mexico desert. Henniger shifted in his seat, turning half way towards the couple behind him.

"We're goin' to a little motel, 'bout twenty miles off the main Highway here. Got one of the big boys from the Top wants to see ya Mr Oakes. We stay there tonight, then fly ya down to San Diego from Albuquerque in the morning. Ya gotta be there for briefing Sunday noon."

"What'd I tell you, Boysie honey? Albuquerque! Yuck!" said Chicory.

Boysie reflected that all this piddling about was seriously cutting into his living-it-up time. But then, without the piddling about there might not be any time in which to live it up.

"Incidentally, Miss Triplehouse, you'll be able to fly back direct to New York," continued Henniger. "You've done your job and you'll be contacted on return."

"To hell with that!" Chicory's reaction was violent. "I'm goin' on down to San Diego."

"Sorry, Miss Triplehouse, them's my orders." Henniger was firm.

"I'm going on down to San Diego of my own accord then. Vacation."

"You'll go straight back to New York."

"Now look here ... I can do just as I goddam please. I'm a free agent."

"There is no such thing as a *free* agent." The voice was clipped. Final. The conversation had finished as far as Henniger was concerned. Chicory opened her mouth to speak again, then thought better of it. They had pulled off the main Freeway, and seemed to be hurtling unsteadily along a disused stage coach track. Boysie put out his hand and felt Chicory's hot in his. He could sense her blazing. "Why don't you do something about the little shit?" she hissed in Boysie's ear. Boysie considered the situation and decided that there was very little he could do in the circumstances. The atmosphere was not unlike that of a Mothers' Union Meeting at which the chairwoman had just advocated free love.

Fifteen minutes later they were back on the main highway. No one had spoken since Chicory's hiss. She still simmered, while Boysie remained perplexed. The two men in front seemed quite at ease. A notice on their right said, "Rio Grande Motel One Mile. TV. Pool. Air conditioning. Twenty Units."

The Rio Grande Motel was a two-tiered, pink stucco monstrosity trying to look like a hacienda, built to form three sides of a square. It gave the impression of being a tired oasis in the midst of the hot dry prairie.

"Looks a bit seedy," ventured Boysie.

"Old guy who built it thought he'd gotta gold mine—catch passing trade too tired to go on to Albuquerque. Just didn't pay off. Who's goin' to stay in a place like this when they can get the real thing in half an hour's driving?" replied Henniger. "Anyhow, he's got the trade today. We've taken the whole place justa be on the safe side."

They began to disembark from the car. The patio was deserted. The pool looked stagnant. "The living desert," breathed Boysie, and, trying to make light of what promised to be a very fraught situation, began to sing softly, "There's a small motel . . ."

"Cut it, will ya, Oakes . . ." said Henniger sharply.

"Now wait a minute . . ." Boysie started, then he felt the power of the steely eyes and thought again. He much preferred the quiet efficiency of Lofrese and the cheery bombast of the late lamented Joe Siedler to this kind of treatment.

"Not here then. Not yet," said the grey-haired man: the first words he had spoken, except for a short oath when the driver of a jumbo-sized convertible had cut in on them just outside Santa Rosa.

"Didn't expect them ta be." Henniger was looking around him. "Flight's not due till eleven." Boysie glanced at his watch. It was only eight-thirty and already, standing out in the open, the sun was beginning to fry the back of his neck.

"Where the hell's that old fool." Henniger raised his voice to a bellow. "Hey, Pop, where are ya! Pop!"

"OK. No need ta shout. I kin hear ya." The old man came hobbling round the corner of the hacienda—a walking image of the old gag about 'that's waar the horse goes': a beanpole in tight Levis, with a face held together by deep wrinkles and thick white stubble. He regarded the group with unflattering suspicion.

"These are the people I told ya 'bout," said Henniger with a gesture towards Boysie and Chicory.

"Thought th'was gonna be three more men."

"Other two'll be over later."

The old man spat at a crop of weeds. Boysie could have sworn they wilted. "OK, you're payin'," said the proprietor.

"The luggage is in the trunk." Henniger walked slowly back to the car, keys in hand. The oldster continued to look at Boysie and Chicory. Boysie began to penetrate the mental processes which lay behind the look. The only people likely to stay at this place were couples bent on adultery. The old horror was obviously adept at spotting naughty weekenders. Bet he bleeds them white, thought Boysie.

"Ya together? Or are ya separates?" asked the nasty old man.

Before Boysie could make an indignant reply, Chicory startled him:

"Together," she said, meaning every word of it.

"Hey now..." Henniger stood up quickly from behind the car.

"Together!" repeated Chicory, looking the security man full in the eyes.

"Are you sure that's . . .?" Henniger was smiling at her: putting on a little style.

"Together!"

Henniger's smile curdled. He continued to look at her. The grey-haired man shuffled his feet. Henniger capitulated, nodded, and bent down again to unlock the boot. Pleased, Boysie turned to smile at Chicory, intending it to be a look of mingled warmth and desire. Ludicrously, he mistimed the turn and cannoned, undignified and hard, into the grey-haired man, who had been moving behind him towards Henniger.

"I'm so sorry." Boysie noticed that the grey-haired man had a slight accent which suited the smooth manner. European, possibly Italian, he thought.

The proprietor made a production number out of carrying the luggage: the limp and heavy breathing coming much into play as he led them across the patio to a ground floor room under the cloister in the central part of the jaded building. The motel room was strangely familiar to Boysie: the large bed, with curved lamps like horns sprouting from either side of the head, armchair, built-in wardrobe, towering television, the pitcher of water with the wax drum for ice cubes, and the compact bathroom with shower, wash basin and lavatory. It was exactly as he had imagined it from Mr Fleming's novels—right down to the strip of hygienic paper sealing the lavatory seat, and the impregnated tissue for polishing shoes.

"Big man should be here 'bout noon," said Henniger from the doorway. "If ya want anythin' just ring. We'll be along when he needs ya. OK?"

"Fine. Thank you," said Boysie. The door closed on them.

"Well?" Boysie smiled.

"Well my arse," said Chicory, not unpleasantly.

"What?"

"You weren't going to do a thing about it, were you?"

"About what?"

"About anything. I had to put my foot down. What the heck? What gives with those guys? They own you or something, Boysie? Gee, did you make me mad. Letting them tell *me* what to do? Couldn't you have said something?"

"Look, Chicory darling. Honestly, I'm sorry." Boysie was floundering. "I'm in a very tricky position. I'm supposed to do what these people tell me. Under orders."

"Orders! I suppose you'll get chewed up for sharing this room with me then?" She was piqued.

Boysie grinned. "Oh definitely," he said, putting on his county drawl. "Be booted out of the hunt; blackballed from every decent club; put on the undesirable list by the debs' mums; won't even be allowed to exhibit at Cruft's . . ."

"What the hell are you talking about, you crazy Englishman? Is that Limey humour or something?"

"Indubitably." He laughed, then stopped, his face grave. She was sitting on the edge of the bed, looking up at him with those great almond eyes glittering a kind of violence. They stayed there, staring at each other: taking in long draughts of the emotion which leaped between them. Boysie moved over to the bed as she put up her arms, stretching forward in invitation, with head back and the tight orbs of her breasts standing out inside her sweater as though straining to break through and encompass him. He felt her close, her lips on his, and the same spiral intertwining they had experienced in New York. She was running her hands over him as they rocked back on to the bed. They rolled over once: then, together, they were clawing at each other's clothes, stripping one another, hurling garments from them in a frenzy of need.

This was wholly animal—as he knew it would be with Chicory. All hunger and the desire for a complete uninhibited

73

satisfying of the sensual appetite. They thrust at each other, and bit, and scratched, hanging on as though this was a wild struggle for possession, not the free mutual granting of their bodies. Sweat poured from them, between them, adding fuel to the physical momentum of the act. When it was finished, and they had both stopped shivering from the long ecstatic shudder that was their peak, Chicory continued to run her hands expertly and smoothly over his body. A long time later, she spoke:

"Aren't bodies wonderful, Boysie? Aren't they just wonderful things?"

"Be lost without 'em." He couldn't resist it. She chuckled, grateful that he had broken the tension, and kissed him on the nose.

"May I tell you," she said, "that you are now on my highly recommended list."

"You get the full four-star treatment and a whole chapter to yourself in my autobiography."

"That won't be an autobiography, honey; that'll be a standard work of reference." She looked at him, her eyes doing a complicated tango. "You've been around, haven't you, Boysie baby?"

"I have, as they say, had my moments." He bent over her again, but she gently pushed him away.

"Not now, darling. We'll have tonight. I need a shower."

They took the shower together, like children playing at water carnivals; rubbed each other down, and rummaged in their cases for clean clothes.

"I feel great." Chicory was standing in the middle of the room, legs apart, hands on her hips, dressed only in tight white briefs and bra. "How about some coffee?"

"All right, but get some of those clothes on first. If the old man brings it, you could give him a heart attack. I can vouch for it, you look gorgeous."

"Nuts. Ring down and get some coffee."

Boysie was juggling with the telephone. "Damn thing seems dead. Can't get a peep."

"Let Mama have a go." Chicory came over and fiddled with

74

the instrument. "No. Looks as if it's out of order. Can't say I'm surprised, the joint's falling to bits. See that plaster?"

"I'll give the old-timer a shout." Boysie fastened the waist-band of his second best slacks and went over to the door. At first he thought it was just jammed; then his heart started to take on the trip-hammer pound. The door was locked. From the outside. Somewhere in the back of his consciousness, Boysie tried to remember something: something that had half come through to him as they had been making love.

"What's wrong, Boysie? What's the matter?"

"The door. They've locked the bloody door. My God . . ."

He made a dive across the room towards the television where his charcoal slacks had landed when Chicory wrenched them from his legs, kicking to be unfettered, as they fought for naked-ness on the bed. His hands scrabbled at the material, but he knew already. It had gone. He felt the muscles twitching on the left side of his mouth, the tremors, the blood draining from his face, and the twisting in his guts.

"Boysie, what the hell is it? Why?" Chicory was close to him now, a hand on his arm.

"My gun. The bastards have taken my gun." He could have been a small boy running to Mum because the game of Cow-boys and Indians had gone all wrong. He remembered the grey-haired man bumping into him—that's when they lifted the weapon.

"They've locked us in here and pinched my bleedin' gun." His right fist was balled, punching into his thigh.

"Your? Boysie, what is all this? For . . ."

"Oh, great balls of fire," he moaned, his knees beginning to give way. "Great fuming, fornicating balls of rancid fire." Boysie buckled on to the bed. "What d'you think it means? Those characters are the boys who sent the two gorillas to lug me out of the New Weston: the twits who parcelled up that fancy snake. They're no more security men than my . . ."

"Oh gawd! You mean they're baddies, not goodies?"

"Just that." He nodded.

"For real, Boysie?"

"For all time real."

Boysie looked up to meet the fear in Chicory's face.

"What'll they . . .?"

For her sake, he made an effort: "Oh you'll be all right. They won't do anything to you."

"Please." She was biting her lip and shaking her head from side to side. "What's going on? For Pete's sake what's going on?" The voice ascending the scale. "Myself, I can look after. Anything, I can cope with, and anyone, if I know what's going on. But no one has told me a thing. Just wait till I get back to that bastard Max." From outside came the sound of a car: the slamming of doors; voices, cheery, normal, floating in with the sheets of sunlight through the slits in the venetian blinds. Boysie hauled himself off the bed and went over to the window, prising fingers between two slats of the plastic blind, pushing his face close and looking out. A blue Packard was parked next to the red Mustang. The voices had faded now, and the patio was deserted, wrapped in a warm siesta silence broken occasionally by the wrumm of a car passing on the road a few yards away.

"They're not going to be fool enough to leave the keys hanging around just for us, you dope." Chicory's fear was turning into angry spirit. Boysie looked round the room, his eyes settling on the bathroom window. All the windows had an outer protective covering of fine mesh—a barricade against insects and the night creatures of the desert—but these would be easily removable. If they could get to the road, perhaps a passing car? As though reading his thoughts, Chicory shattered the idea at conception.

"Don't think of running. There's an awful lot of desert out there."

Boysie knew she was right. Anyway they would be watching the door, that was certain. The chances of reaching the road were about as slim as extra-thin rice paper. He returned to the bed, sat down and put his head in his hands.

"That bloody Mostyn," he breathed. "That super bastard Mostyn."

With a little effort he might even bring himself to believe that Mostyn had, by some foul plan, pushed him, on purpose, into this predicament.

"Wait." Chicory motioned silence. Someone was coming down the cloister outside. The shadows of Henniger and the grey-haired man passed the window.

"How about jumping them?" Chicory whispered: her eyes wide and questioning.

It was too late. A key turned in the lock and the two men stood in the doorway.

"He wants to see ya now," said Henniger.

"Bloody Commie bastard," was all Boysie could think up at short notice.

"It finally penetrated, huh? Get that Cirio? A real smart guy, this Limey agent. He finally caught on."

"Smart," said Cirio, "Very smart, Ritzy." There was a gun in his hand. "We would like you to come with us, please." He spoke politely, as though showing a couple to a table in his club. "I'm afraid madam will have to wait here. For the time being, anyway. And really I wouldn't recommend trying to run for it. Both sides of the building are watched. Actually, you have met the gentlemen who are performing that service for us—in the New Weston the other night. One of them is most anxious to see you again, Mr Oakes. You hurt his arm somewhat. Luckily, he is ambidextrous."

"Aw cut it, Cirio, they're waiting." Ritzy Henniger turned to the girl. "Ya look cute, babe, wouldn't mind a whirl myself." Chicory crossed her hands over her breasts, realising that she was still only dressed in the revealing undies.

Cirio made a waving motion with the gun. "If you don't mind, Mr Oakes."

Boysie got up: trembling, unsteady. Chicory's hand brushed his arm.

"Careful, Boysie darling. Please."

Boysie took a lungful of air. His head felt as if it was doing an energetic butterfly stroke through liquid treacle. "I'll be back," he managed.

"I sincerely hope so," said Henniger, smiling with his mouth only.

Outside it was really hot. Danger often turns the mind towards trivialities, and Boysie considered that it must be at least ninety-two degrees in the shade. They led him down the cloister to a door at the end of the block. Room 12. The unit was similar to the one that he was sharing with Chicory. A shade darker, but perhaps that was due to coming in from the harsh light, or because the bathroom door was shut. From behind it came the sound of splashing water and a man's voice singing softly. Boysie had a strange feeling that he had heard the voice before. Through the murk he could distinguish the figure of a man sitting in the armchair by the television. The figure moved slightly and spoke.

"Mr Boysie Oakes; I am most happy to make your acquaintance. Gentlemen, would you adjust the blinds, please, Mr Oakes and I would like to see one another." The accent was thick: whipped cream forced through gauze. Boysie unconsciously noted that there was no trace of the American twang. This one had learned his English in Europe. Cirio opened the blind and took up a position against the wall, behind Boysie. Ritzy Henniger sat on the bed. The man in the armchair was ageless, looking to Boysie, like a fat, elegant rich pastry, ripe to ooze its filling. The skin visible on his hands, arms (he wore a blue short-sleeved sports shirt and slacks that bulged opulently around the midriff), neck, and face had that off-white flabby look and a powdery texture; the hair, thin and combed back from the brow in a silky silver sheen. The one bizarre touch—giving the man a curious, doll-like expression—were the eyebrows: full, heavy and dark: a startling contrast. He was drumming on the edge of the armchair with a set of puffy fingers which looked like eclairs ready for the icing. The other hand lay immobile in his lap. From under the George Robey eyebrows, two abnormally small eyes held Boysie with a steady, hypnotic gaze.

"You will want to know what all this is about, Boysie Oakes. And I do not blame you for that. In fact, I think we can give

78

you a pretty extensive picture. I think we owe that to you at least. There would be no danger in that." The eyes were static, unblinking. "No danger, because, Mr Boysie Oakes, you will not be around to pass on any information to your friends in London. Or San Diego. Or anywhere. If you want to talk, you can perhaps chat up St Peter, or the nasty gentleman with the horns and pitchfork. Do you believe in St Peter? I find him harder to comprehend than the Dark Angel—there is certainly a Dark Angel, don't you think?"

"Do you mind very much if I sit down?" It was about the most foolish thing Boysie had said that day. But a man is not often sentenced to death in such an off-hand manner.

"Oh, I am sorry, Mr Oakes. A chair for Mr Oakes, Cirio."

Cirio moved a stand chair from the window corner and pushed it behind Boysie's knees. He sank gratefully on to its hard seat and, through the series of black concentric circles which appeared to be his brain, tried to concentrate on what the fat pudding was saying.

"In my particular line I am a rather important person. My name is Gorilka. Dr Gorilka." He reached out to the little coffee table on the right of the chair, picked up a small, flat, black and green box and took out a long Russian cigarette—two-thirds cardboard tube and one-third tobacco. With immense care, he crimped the end of the tube. Henniger leaned forward from the bed and lit the cigarette for him.

"In Russia, they laugh at my name." He gave a highly bronchial, chesty wheeze which Boysie took to be the progenitorial spasm of a laugh. "They think it is funny because in the Ukraine, Gorilka is a kind of vodka. I do not drink, incidentally. That is a useless piece of information given gratis, but I am told it renders the joke about my name even funnier. To Ukrainians, that is."

Boysie saw nothing hilarious about the name, or the fact that Gorilka was TT.

"In my own country," Gorilka continued, allowing his mouth to hang open and pushing out a cloud of smoke in a short, quick exhalation, "I am a Doctor of Law, a Doctor of

Philosophy, a Doctor of Medicine and a Doctor of Languages. So you see I am not exactly without an academic background. For the past year I have been in this country—incognito, of course—organising a particular project on behalf of . . . well . . . The Project is quite simple. Quite clear cut. But when you arrived, it was decided to add a small refinement. An extra safety precaution." He drew in on the cigarette. "Our job was, first, to get hold of you. My friends here were given this simple assignment." The hand rose, indicating Ritzy and Cirio: a gesture bordering on disdain. "As you know, things went wrong, and Mr . . . er . . . Mr Henniger thought it might be a good idea to eliminate you altogether." He gave a weary sigh. "I must apologise for that, Mr Oakes. The attempt was rather crude and haphazard. You will be eliminated, of course, but it must be done privately, quietly, with taste (I think reptiles such tasteless creatures, don't you?), and, of course, without any witnesses."

Boysie was rapidly falling into a state of mind which refused to accept reality. "But why me? I'm not important. Surely?" He was not altogether with this conversation.

Gorilka smiled—it was the look morticians engineer on the faces of corpses. "You would be suprised to learn just how important you have become. Let me try and show you." He turned his head towards the bathroom door and raised his voice: "Are you coming? He's here. He wants to meet you."

"Ready in a moment." The voice from behind the door was very familiar. Boysie's mind sidetracked, trying to work out where he heard it before. Then the bathroom door opened.

For about fifteen seconds Boysie did not recognise the man who had come into the room. He knew him well, but just could not place the face. Slowly it hit him. It was crazy. He was seeing things. He was looking at himself.

"Hallo," said the man. Even the voice was Boysie's; and the friendly smile. Grief, he looked at this in the mirror every morning—wasn't that enough? The man came towards him, hand outstretched. "This is very odd, isn't it? Meeting one-self?"

The room began to fog up. Boysie could only think that this was his *doppelgänger*: the apparition one saw just before death. Gorilka had said that he was about to be eliminated, and by some weird psychic phenomenon Boysie was face to face with himself. In a moment there would be oblivion.

"It is really quite amazing," said Gorilka.

"Kinda spooky," said Henniger.

Boysie looked into his own face, and the flesh and blood of his own face looked back at him.

IV – SOLEV

NORMALITY was returning. Boysie was conscious of discrepancies. For one thing, he and the *doppelgänger* were not wearing the same clothes, though there was no doubt that they shopped at the same places. The check trousers and black polo neck were definitely Jaeger. Boysie looked at the ensemble with some satisfaction. He had the identical things back in the flat off Chesham Place. He reflected that he had always considered them rather hip.

"How do you like your double, Mr Oakes?" Gorilka heaved him back to the matter in hand. "That's who he is. Your double. Did you think it was the end? That he was your *doppelgänger*?"

"How the hell . . .?"

". . . Did I know?" The creamy smile was set into the doughy face. "If you had the chance to be around as long as I have, you would begin to recognise the signs. You are not unintelligent . . ."

"Thank you very much." Boysie's terror was now seasoned with arrogance.

Gorilka took an impatient breath and started again. "You are not unintelligent, but you have a transparent mind. This gentleman, your own familiar, is Mr Vladimir Solev. Vladimir . . ." He gestured: an introductory palm flapping between the two men. . . . Vladimir, Mr Boysie Oakes. Boysie, if I may be allowed to call you so, Mr Vladimir Solev."

The situation was so macabre that Boysie could only say: "How do you do?"

Solev grinned, took Boysie's hand in his, shook it, and said warmly (in Boysie's voice), "How do you do? I really am so glad to meet you at last. I feel that we are quite old friends."

"I bet you do." Incredulous.

"Before you two start falling on each other's necks," Gorilka was impatient, "I still have one or two things to tell Mr Oakes. You will have already come to certain conclusions, my dear sir. Mr Solev is quite a property, and you will have, rightly, deduced that he is going on to San Diego as yourself. It will be Mr Solev, and not you, who will be present at the *Playboy* firing trials on Monday; and it will be Mr Solev who will be able to give great assistance to our operatives in San Diego in connection with the firing trials. We have a few surprises planned for Monday."

Boysie was beginning to come out of his bewilderment. Though death hovered near, he had just noticed that Solev's face was grave. As the creamy gent spoke, Boysie saw that Solev's mouth was tipping up in a series of jerks; beads of perspiration were forming above the eyes; starting to saturate his eyebrows. There were signs that Boysie knew well. Intimately. Vladimir Solev was afraid. Come to that, considered Boysie, so was he. Bloody terrified. But Solev's fear might be put to some concrete use. Gorilka was still speaking. "It would have been quite easy for us simply to get rid of you. Liquidate you, would probably be a better phrase in view of your past activities. But I felt that it would be a nice touch to allow the two of you to meet. To let you talk. To let Vladimir here put the finishing touches to his excellent impersonation. I mean, it would be foolish to turn down such an opportunity."

Boysie was still staring at Solev. The likeness was uncanny. Solev caught his eye and smiled nervously.

"They have done a good job on him, don't you think? Much time and energy has been spent on perfecting the likeness; but an hour alone with you will be of great value. Good?" He leaned forward. Henniger stood up, and Cirio moved closer to Boysie's chair. Gorilka looked at his watch. "It saddens me to tell you this, Mr Oakes, but you have roughly one hour left to live. It will be spent here, in this room with your new-found friend, Vladimir. I trust that you will be able to help him. And please do not try anything foolish. Vladimir is armed; so are the guards, and they will only shoot to wound. I might as well tell you now that the manner of your demise depends on how much value you are to Vladimir. If you help him, it will be quick and comparatively painless. If you—how do you Americans put it?" He looked towards Henniger.

"Clam up," said Henniger without expression.

"Yes. If you clam up, it will be very painful; and it will take a long time. So please do not be silly."

Boysie still could not really believe all this talk about being killed. He feared pain and death more than anything, but still retained man's essential optimism that it could never happen to him. He remembered Chicory.

"What about the girl?" he asked.

"Ah yes, the girl." Gorilka inspected his finger nails frowning.

"Her destiny is in your hands also," he said, cryptically. "So help friend Vladimir, eh? Now we go to lunch. I will see that some coffee is sent in to you. Have a nice chat."

Gorilka eased himself out of the chair. For the first time, Boysie saw that he was partially crippled, walking with a slow lumber, leaning heavily on a thick stick. Cirio came forward and took the fat man's arm, guiding him towards the door. As they reached the threshold, Gorilka turned, looked at Solev and spat out a sentence in rapid Russian. The frightened look was more deeply set in Vladimir's eyes.

"*Da*," replied Vladimir.

Even Boysie knew that *da* meant "yes". "Yes what?" he asked himself starting to think how best he could use their mutual fear.

"THAT'S A Makarov, isn't it?" Boysie was looking at the compact little automatic pistol that Solev held loosely in his lap.

"Yes. Very accurate weapons. Like to have a look? Oh no. Perhaps not." Solev had been about to hand the gun across to the Englishman. He looked embarrassed. "I'm sorry. I keep forgetting. What I said just now was perfectly true: you really do seem like an old friend." He looked at Boysie, the eyes troubled. "Please, this is not my fault."

"No, I don't suppose it is, but that doesn't help me, does it?" said Boysie curtly from the edge of the bed. Solev was in the armchair recently vacated by Gorilka. Between them, on the small table, stood two plastic cups soiled with the dregs of their coffee. Boysie had no idea how he was going to play this. All he knew was that there must be a way out; though he had the distinct notion that by some strange chemical process his whole internal complex was being quickly changed into calves'-foot jelly. "You know," he said, trying to sound at ease in the face of the odds stacked against him, "it really is fantastic. You've even got my voice. I suppose you were educated in England?"

"Never been there in my life. I was born in Moscow. I'm five days older than you by the way."

"Never been to England? You're joking. How the . . .?" Boysie vaguely remembered reading somewhere (he thought in Gunther's *Inside Russia Today*, which had been on the Department's prescribed reading list) that Muscovite radio announcers, who had never been outside their own country, could imitate almost every kind of British or American accent.

"Until eight months ago I was just, how would *you* say it, 'an ordinary man in the street'? My father was a doctor. I suppose I grew up with the revolution, but I'm not very good at politics." He gave a half-hearted laugh. "Just did as I was told. I've always been one for keeping out of trouble."

Boysie tried to look understanding. Solev went on, "Since the war I've been working in industry—on the clerical side, of course." A hint of pride in his voice as he added, "Last year I was promoted Assistant Deputy Head Clerk at the tractor factory in Volgograd—you know, used to be Stalingrad."

"Bully for you," said Boysie without much enthusiasm. "How the blazes did you manage to get into this business then?" His thoughts whipped over the time when he had been recruited to the Department. He had been the owner of a down-at-heel cafe and aviary then; the most unlikely person to get mixed up with the secret war of plot and counter-plot.

Solev shifted uneasily. "I don't suppose it would do any harm to tell you." He kept biting at his lower lip, rolling the red skin out slowly from between his teeth. "But there are some questions I must ask you."

"You'll have time," Boysie was desperately fumbling for some clue, some fact on which he might be able to work: a lever to jemmy his way out of unthinkable death.

"Oh well. All right." It was obvious that Solev was pleased at the opportunity to talk about himself. "It started one day last winter. Nothing unusual except that we had a visiting deputation of officers from the Defence Ministry. You know the kind of thing: they're shown round the factory; make speeches to the workers." Boysie nodded, he could imagine the dreary political round and comic task. "One of them was a very important name in security circles. I'd never heard of him then, of course. Have you heard of Khavichev?"

"Who hasn't?" said Boysie. "The man's a legend. Actually he's quite respected on our side of the fence." It was really big stuff if Khavichev was concerned.

"That's interesting. They really respect him?"

"We still manage to keep our sense of chivalry, you know. Give credit where credit's due," said Boysie pompously. "What about Khavichev?"

"They all came into our room—where we were working— and Khavichev just stood there looking at me. Nearly had a fit. Went quite white." Solev's face crumpled into a smile and he chuckled. "Looking back, it was quite funny. Frightening at the time, though. Place seemed to go mad. One minute I was preparing a report for my superior; the next, they were dragging me into the Comrade Director's office. Khavichev wouldn't let me speak to anyone. Two of his men with me all the time. *All* the time. It was very embarrassing. Kept asking them what it was all about, but they wouldn't tell me a thing. Then some uniformed police arrived with a van. Took me to the airport— outriders, all sorts of precautions—and flew me to Moscow. They had me in Security Headquarters for two days. Question after question."

"Question after question. Fancy!" Boysie tried to sound suitably bland. "Why?"

"It's obvious, isn't it?"

"He didn't think you were . . .?" Boysie began tentatively.

"You. Yes." Solev clinched it. "You can't really blame him, can you? I'm pretty shaken myself, now that we're face to face."

Boysie nodded. "Bet he was mad when he found he'd made a mistake."

"I gather he was at first. Then he decided he could use me. They moved me out of headquarters and into a villa in the Lenin Hills. Do you know Moscow? . . . No, of course you don't. It's a nice area, the Lenin Hills. Near the University. I'd never known such luxury. Magnificent—everything a man could wish for. Everything. If you follow me."

"I'm way ahead of you." Boysie was thinking of the first time Mostyn had taken him to the flat—which was to become his own—off Chesham Place. That had been a new experience of sumptuousness for him.

"Khavichev came to see me. Apologised for the inconvenience, and told me that I was the double of a very important British agent."

"He called *me* important?" Boysie was not unhappy at the thought.

"Of course. You *are* important."

"Oh come off it." Inexplicably, Boysie felt himself going a light pink.

"No. Really. You should see the information they have about you—the dossier they have compiled. Anyone in the game would be proud of such a dossier being drawn up by the opposition."

"No?"

"Yes. Films, tape recordings, your habits. We have similar tastes, by the way. That nice girl Elizabeth, you were seeing so much of. The secretary with the Board of Trade. Did you . . ."?

"Yes," said Boysie. "Frequently."

"Oh good. She looked super. They had some good movie film of you together. They really have an awful lot of you." He faltered, realising that he had shunted from the main story-line. "Khavichev said that he could make me a Hero of the Republic if I worked hard. Well, everyone would like to be a hero, wouldn't they? Secretly, that's what we all want. He promised me all kinds of things . . ." Boysie's thoughts slewed back to the time when Mostyn had offered him the earth; promised him riches beyond the dreams of Archie Rice if he would take on that special formidable job with the Department.

Solev continued: "And I worked. My life I worked. I knew some English. They taught me more: then gave me your voice . . ."

"That slays me. The voice bit. How . . .?"

"Deep hypnosis mostly. In a sound-proof cubicle at the University. They say the brain is at its most receptive under hypnosis: nothing else can get in the way. Days on end I did it. Lying there while a tape-recorder played back your voice—how you sound your vowels and consonants."

"A touch of the Professor Higgins!" murmured Boysie.

"Oh no, Professor Engler was my chief language instructor —brilliant man—used to give me post-hypnotic suggestions: when I woke up I would pronounce things your way. And I did." He shrugged, scratching the back of his neck. "Then there were lists of the words you used most; phrases; expressions. I spoke nothing but English after that interview with Khavichev. Couldn't speak English in any other way now. Does it really sound like you?"

"It's like being a perishing ventriloquist without knowing it."

"Oh, then they taught me to walk like you—all your mannerisms. I ate your favourite food, I must thank you for that, by the way. Never knew what food was until I started this training." He looked, to Boysie, like a puppy begging for compliments. "Well, you can see the result: I became you!" Solev spread his hands expansively like a conjuror ending a smart trick. Boysie realised that both the look and the gesture were typical of himself.

"I believe you did." A slim plan was germinating in Boysie's mind. It was mad, but it might just work. He must not panic now.

"Clever buggers, aren't they?" said Boysie.

"Oh, they're clever enough. Never underestimate them, Boysie. We must never do that." Solev was still sweating.

"I wonder," said Boysie, "if they really have turned you into another me. Completely. There are so many similarities. You were forced into all this. So was I."

"Forced? You were?"

"Against my better judgement—as they say. Really, Vladimir, tell me honestly. Do you like the job, or is it a right drag?"

Solev looked like a trapped animal; refusing to meet Boysie's eyes squarely. "I enjoyed the training." Apprehensive. "I enjoyed the challenge of becoming you. I can honestly say I enjoyed that." Recovering a little of his unsteady poise.

"But the special training. What about the special training? Getting ready for this operation. Going out on a limb. On your own. Do you find all this excites you? Or . . .?"

"I'm sorry about *you* . . ." He was evading the issue—clumsily. "Now really, I must ask you . . ."

"Please!" Boysie was pushing his advantage. "This is very important to me. Your heart? Is your heart really in this? Or are you like me?"

"What d'you mean: like you?"

Boysie prepared to play his small trump. He had never told this to a living soul. "I was pressganged into the whole bloody issue. Just like you." His voice was rough in the back of his throat. "I did it mainly for the money. Because I was broke. Because I've always fancied a bit of luxury. They gave *me* the Pygmalion bit as well. Instructors? I know the lot. Ye gods, it's all very well these newspaper people and the writers scribbling away about operatives being ordinary blokes in dirty coats working in scruffy offices—that's a load of old dishwater for a start. Vladimir, our Department has got more tradition than the Guards and the Royal Marines put together, if that means anything to you. Talk about snobbery. When I got into the game —at the training school—there was one chap there wouldn't speak to me for a fortnight when he found out I bought my razor blades at Woolworths. They only take the real cut glass under normal circumstances. Won't touch anyone unless he's got the right background. I didn't even know what a public school looked like so they had to lay on a whole course for me—build a nice genteel façade." He grinned at the memory. "I must say they gave me the best; they even got Ken Tynan—in the flesh, mate—to come and talk to me about Drama. Nice bloke Ken, didn't understand half of what he was on about, but he's a nice bloke. . . . I had just about the most exclusive short course in the Arts and table manners . . ." he broke off and leaned forward, fingertips touching Solev's left wrist. "You said just now that we all secretly wanted to be heroes. I suppose that's true, but we all know what we really are, and I'm not brave. If you want to know, I'm a flipping coward. I didn't even do most of the things they credit me with. Inside I'm just a churning cold-sweat flavoured blancmange. I know psychiatrists who'd pay good money to have a go at me." He was really away now. "Honestly, Vladimir, I think you *are* like me: scared bloody stiff. And if you are, I can tell you, now's the time to kick it—get the hell out of it. I should have got out when I had the chance: gone and been a road sweeper or something—security officer in a supermarket. I'd have been a wow in a supermarket, catching kids knocking off the cereal packets for the plastic gifts inside. That's just about my mark; cereal minder."

"But you . . ." Solev's mouth was open. Hanging.

"Oh, it's all right when you're not on a job. When you're on stand-down, then it's great: the car and the flat, plenty of money, noshing it up, and the birds, the dolly, dolly birds. But most of the time—on your own—it's pure palpitating agony. The anxiety: I'm not kidding, Vladimir. . . ."

Solev's hands were shaking. A low groan of recognition came struggling from strangled vocal chords. "I want to be sick," moaned Solev.

"How the hell do you think I feel? All the time I want to be sick."

"But I couldn't get out of it. Even if I wanted to."

"And you do want to." A statement.

"With our lot, if you don't do as they say, it's the salt mines, or worse. . . ."

"Schtucksvillesky."

"I feel dreadful, Boysie. And what's it going to be like when they've . . . When you've gone?" His look was one Boysie knew well enough—despair. "I'm lucky to have got this far. Once I'm really on my own, I'll fold up. I'll just fold up. But what else could I do?"

"I know." Boysie felt his breathing ease a fraction. "You'd probably get through this one all right. But then there'll be another; and another. It's like blackmail, and the end is going to be the same. When I think about it I could die." He realised, his stomach dropping about six inches, that the words were colourfully appropriate.

"What can I do?" Solev looked ghastly.

"What do you want most in the world?"

Silence. Then: "Before all this happened, in Russia, I thought I was happy—just doing my work. I'd never married but that didn't worry me. Always enough in the samovar. The borsch had plenty of sausage in it. Now, it's no good. I know I can't do this kind of work. I feel like a parachutist all the time —and I hate heights. During the training I learned a lot about England. I've become an Englishman. There were television films and things. I was taught to think like an Englishman." He made a peculiar noise, half-snort, half-laugh. "The questions I wanted to ask. They had nothing to do with being you. I wanted to hear if the Beatles were still top of the hit parade, and how Ena Sharples was getting on in *Coronation Street*, and that nice doctor, what's his name? Kildare . . ."

"He's American, and you can probably see whose death-bed he's attending by just switching that thing on." Boysie nodded towards the television.

"Really, Vladimir, in our kind of society you just don't watch *Coronation Street* or *Doctor Kildare*. You don't admit it anyway. It's all *Panorama* and *Monitor*, Richard Dimbleby and those plays that don't have proper endings. . . ."

"What about David Frost?"

"The satirical bloke?"

"I think he's got guts. To say the kind of thing he says about your government and the royal family, he must have guts."

"They haven't really taught you much about our way of life, have they? I mean, they should know that the Royals aren't 'in' any more; and the government is never 'in', let's face it."

"The people don't like the royal family?"

"Well, they don't dislike them. But . . . How can I put it? The gossip columnists love them . . . but, well, all those corgis, and playing hockey on a horse. Actually I met the Duke once. He was jolly nice to me."*

"But if the people don't like them, why don't they revolt?"

"They're revolting enough already."

"I beg your pardon?"

"Never mind. Look, Vladimir. What are we going to do about all this? You'd like to get to England?"

"How could I? We'd never . . ."

"You don't want to go on with this operation?"

"No, of course I don't."

"Then help me. We'll get away together." Boysie reflected that he sounded like a melodramatic hero propositioning the lady of the manor. "Once we're in San Diego I'll see you all right. Have you on a plane in no time. You could be safe in London in a couple of days with no more anxieties. Think of it, mate, London—Big Ben, the Houses of Parliament, Buckingham Palace, Piccadilly, the Law Courts . . . The Tower!" he added tentatively.

Solev swallowed. "Couldn't I go by boat? I loathe flying. I'm always ill and feel awful for days afterwards. I haven't really got over the trip from Moscow yet."

The opposition, thought Boysie, did not know how well they had chosen their man. Boysie and Solev did not just have twin bodies, they had twin neuroses.

"We'll worry about the details when we get there. The thing is, are you coming?"

"It'll mean killing . . . I don't like the idea."

" 'Gainst my principles too," said Boysie. "But for me it's

* See *The Liquidator*.

either kill or be killed. Come to that, it's the same for you as well. Are you with me?"

The moment of indecision seemed infinite. Then Solev nodded. "If I stay with the job I'll end up dead or in Siberia. That's for sure. At least I'll have a chance if I come with you. Anyway, I can't just stand by and let them shoot you? It'd be like killing myself. I've been living your life for months now. What a strange situation."

Ludicrous, thought Boysie, sliding off the bed and starting towards the window. Solev reacted by bringing his gun to the ready.

"For gawd's sake, stop waving that thing about," said Boysie. "You any good with it, by the way?"

"Passable," said Vladimir, looking sheepish.

Outside, the Mustang stood, lonely, in the patio. To the right the water of the swimming pool gleamed green. There was no sign of life.

"They've gone to a restaurant up the road—one Cirio knows," said Solev.

"He said there were guards."

"Yes: two nasty bits of work."

"I've met them."

"One's round the back. They put the other in the room over there."

Solev, standing back from the blind, pointed to the end of the window on the left arm of the building. Boysie was sifting the courses of action.

"How much time have we?"

"Fifteen minutes. Give or take five."

"All right, call that one out of his hidey hole. Tell him you've had some trouble with me—or something. If we can put the guards out of action before the three wise monkeys come back we'll stand a chance. And give me that gun; you're going to do someone a mischief." Solev had been fiddling with the Makarov like a learner gunfighter. He handed over the weapon without a murmur. Boysie felt a pleasant surge of power. Obviously, he was going to be the leader. "OK," he said. "Get him over here," flattening himself against the wall, behind the door, as he had seen it done in B movies.

Solev opened the door, and, raising an arm, called towards the thug's hiding place.

"Hey, you there. Give me a hand will you. He's being a bit difficult." Then, quietly out of the corner of his mouth, "He's coming Boysie. Careful, he's got a gun."

Boysie could hear the man's feet closing with the door, then his voice as he came near.

"What's he up ta, the bastard? I'll fix him. Nearly broke my arm."

"He's out cold. Just want to help shift him." Solev was a diabolical actor, thought Boysie. That last line had been delivered without a trace of realism. Still the hood was no Bernard Levin so it did not matter much.

"Lead me to him," said the gorilla as he came through the door.

"A pleasure," said Boysie, stepping behind him and bringing the pistol butt sharply down on the base of the skull. It was the man with the scar. He stopped; one foot continued to move forward and he collapsed in a gentle flowing movement. Solev came in and closed the door. Boysie took the man's gun—a heavy Stechkin automatic. He made a mental note to report the fact that opposition men in the USA were armed from behind the Iron Curtain. Now with a full complement of weapons, Boysie returned the Marakov to Solev.

"And do be careful with it, Vladimir."

Together, they lugged the guts into the bathroom, stripped the bed, tore the sheets into neat bandages and trussed up the unconscious hood.

A similar procedure worked, just as smoothly, with the second guard, who came to Solev's call like a gun-dog answering his master's whistle. They dumped him, carefully parcelled with bits of sheet, in the shower next to his buddy.

"Couldn't we just call the police?" asked Solev, not anxious to tangle with the trio who would be returning at any minute.

"Best not, if we can help it. Don't want American officialdom creeping in. If we can get hold of the car keys and make it to San Diego, I'll get straight on to our man there. He'll put us right. If we do it the other way, they might keep us languishing in jail for weeks. You never can tell."

"What do we do when they . . .?" Solev froze to the sound of the Packard turning into the patio.

"Oh Christ!" said Boysie, guts atremble. "I was just going to ask if *you* had any ideas."

Boysie should have seen the signs of panic on Solev's face. But the breaking point came unexpectedly. "Shoot it out with them," Solev screeched, a nervous treble.

"Wait, you great nit!"

Boysie was too late. Solev, with his mistimed brashness, had rocketed towards the window, snatched at the venetian blind and fired two rounds before Boysie could stop him. Both shots went wide of Henniger and Cirio who had been in the act of helping the now replete Gorilka from the rear door of the car. Cirio stood indecisive. Henniger moved for cover behind the vehicle as Gorilka, cursing, threw himself back into the car. Thrust into action, Boysie raised the Stechkin and fired three careful shots.

Cirio twisted violently and seemed to be dragged sideways by an invisible hand, his heels rutting into the earth before he hit the ground and lay still. Boysie's left ear sang as Solev fired beside him, the bullet splintering the rear window of the car.

"For crying out loud. Keep that thing away from my ear-hole, you twerp. And keep down," he yelled, alarmed at the hint of hysteria in his own voice.

Something crashed into the door. Henniger was shooting from behind the Packard. Gorilka—Boysie could just see—was trying to crawl out of the far-side door. At that moment, the old motel proprietor came limping, at speed, round the corner of the hacienda. He shouted and Henniger, unnerved, swivelled and loosed off two shots. The old man caught them squarely in the chest, spun against one of the cloister pillars and dropped in an untidy heap.

Boysie fired again, and heard the slug ricochet off the car's bonnet. Gorilka was shouting something—presumably calling for the guards.

"Gunfight in the OK Corral," mused Boysie, feeling surprisingly at ease. The pitched battle seemed completely unreal: blurred. It certainly was not happening to him. Then, just as quickly, he realised that it was very definitely happening to him. Little sewermen began to tie his intestines into running bowlines.

Solev's next shot finished it. The bullet must have gone clean into the petrol tank: a spark igniting the fuel. With a wild whump the Packard became an explosive ball of flame. They saw Henniger raised from the ground, his dying hands thrown up to shield his face. Gorilka stumbled backwards to land, sprawling and splashing, in the swimming pool.

Boysie, partly recovered, had the door open. "You get the keys . . . on Cirio . . . Hurry . . . I'll bring the girl." He ran unsteadily down the cloister to the room which had been a bridal chamber for Chicory and himself. Vaguely, he took in the scurrying figure of Solev making for Cirio's prone body. The whole firefight must have lasted for less than three minutes. The road remained deserted. Boysie reached the door.

"Chicory . . .? You all right?"

"Boysie . . . What's happened?"

The door was still locked and it took Boysie a second to realise that he couldn't open it with his shoulder.

"Stand clear of the door. Stand by the window."

"OK." Hearing her shout from inside, to his right, he put a bullet through the lock. She came to him, pale with fear.

"Quickly. The Mustang."

"Boysie . . . One minute." Only a woman would bother about possessions at a time like this. Chicory disappeared into the room, and returned dragging both the suitcases. Solev was already in the car clutching the key by the time they reached him. As he hustled them in, Boysie noticed the red paintwork was blistered and crumbling from the heat still being generated by the Packard burning four paces away. The engine roared, drowning the screams of Gorilka, still flailing in the pool. With

Boysie, trembling now, at the wheel, the red sports car screeched out towards Highway 66, heading for Albuquerque.

Solev was jammed between the cases in the rear; Chicory beside Boysie. Frightened as she was, the girl executed a series of double-takes between Vladimir and Boysie.

"Most wonderful," said Chicory Triplehouse, oblivious to the fact that she was quoting one of the Immortal Bard's funnier lines.

Boysie felt the delayed shock wrenching his vitals.

Vladimir Solev, nauseated by the task of robbing Cirio's body for the keys, shook horribly and uncontrollably against Chicory's case.

"FELLA'S MAKIN' a cock-up of it. Nothin' cloak and dagger about this operation. Got no right to get mixed up in skulduggery. What the hell's happened to his sense of values."

The Chief was in a high old paddy. Since the arrival of *USS One's* original cablegram, they had met twice to discuss Boysie's position regarding the *Playboy* trials. Now in the early evening, Mostyn had been forced to trace the Chief to his club. The Old Man had been savouring a large whisky and idly turning the pages of the *Security Gazette* while waiting for the urgent telephone call which summoned him, two nights a week, to a villa in Clapham (old habits die hard), when the steward had told him of the Second-in-Command's presence. In the privacy of the Visitor's Room, Mostyn showed him the latest signal, datetimed for noon on that day. It read:

CONTACT WITH 'L' AND FEMALE ESCORT LOST BETWEEN SANTA ROSA NEW MEXICO AND ALBUQUERQUE STOP ABDUCTION FEARED STOP NO TRACE STOP AWAIT INSTRUCTIONS STOP

"Damn sex maniac, probably gone off with the bint. Havin' it off in some cheap hotel. Wastin' the Department's time and money. Keelhaul the bastard when he gets back."

"If I may remind you, sir," Mostyn was grave. "Boysie was

sent on this assignment at your personal request, and there does seem to be something up."

"I'll bet there's somethin' up."

"Seriously, sir, I do think we should take some action."

"Action! What the hell can we do? Yanks won't thank you for signallin' them; tellin' 'em to stop their trials because one of our blokes has gone missin'. It's quite obvious to me. Either some of Oakes' past has caught up with 'im—and that's a risk we've always had to take—or the fella's gone sexually spare and AWOL. Probably turn up in time for the trials with bloody great bags under his eyes and a spot of the tremblin' kneecaps. You'll see."

"I still don't like it, sir."

The Chief turned down the corners of his mouth, placed the tips of his fingers together just below his lower lip, as though in prayer. He remained in this contemplative attitude for about thirty seconds, then he leaned forward prodding Mostyn in the chest with the bony index finger of his right hand.

"All right, Number Two. All right. You don't bloody like it. Well I'll tell you what we bloody do about it. You just go home, pack your special light-bloody-weight airtravel suitcase, book yourself a trip on a 707 to San Di-bleedin'-ago, via San bloody Francisco, and get bloody weavin'. If you don't like it, then you can bloody go out there and keep a bloodshot eye on things your bloody-self. And that's a direct bleedin' order."

Mostyn, who had much work to do in his office, and innumerable private plans—including some unspeakable deviations involving a well-known dancer and the girl in the cash desk of a Chinese restaurant he had just discovered in Hampstead—gave an agonised internal cry. Aloud, he grunted "Boysie Oakes." He made the name sound impressively obscene.

THEY TOOK turns to drive the racy little Mustang along the Interstate Highway—stopping only for petrol, coffee and hamburgers (Boysie's stomach now right out of control), Coca-Cola and the natural needs. Some of the fear was sweated from them along the burning roads. Chicory was told the basic facts surrounding the fracas at the *Rio Grande*, and, for the thirteenth time, Vladimir assured Boysie that he had no idea how the opposition planned to disrupt Monday's *Playboy-Trepholite* firing trials.

In Phoenix, Arizona, they saw the headlines—TRIPLE SLAYING AT NEW MEXICO MOTEL.

"They don't mention Gorilka, or the couple we popped into the shower," said Boysie, reading the story.

That could only mean one thing. Gorilka and his brace of gunmen were still at large. An extra needle of worry performed a painful series of cross-stitches in the corner of Boysie's conscience.

They reached San Diego at four-thirty on the Saturday afternoon, pulled up in the forecourt of a double-decked Sleepy Bear motel sporting a 'Vacancies' sign, and trotted wearily into the reception office. Way back on the other side of the Arizona State Line they had decided that, once in San Diego, it would be best to check into a motel before Boysie went solo to present the facts, and the news about Solev, to Commander Braddock-Fairchild—Priscilla's sea-dog dad.

Boysie and Chicory registered in their own names; Solev with a notable flourish, signed himself Bernard Oakes—the only way they could surmount the startling double trouble. The impassive manager looked them up and down and slammed three keys on to the counter:

"Be thirty bucks in advance. Rooms are on the second floor." His eyes hovered over Chicory who took a deep breath. "29, 30, 31."

"I beg your pardon?" Said Chicory, much on her dignity.

"Room numbers 29, 30 and 31," said the Manager without a smile.

"Oh. For a moment I thought you were being insulting," said Chicory with a charming wiggle. "Come gentlemen."

V − B + P + T = C

WHEN the moon comes up over San Diego, people smile and say: "M G M is on location tonight." The atmosphere is tropical, luxurious, expensive; cushioned on warm air, zephyr-rocked palms and fine dry sand. To the uncommitted observer, it has the lush, unreal look of a movie set geared for glorious Technicolor. Gazing out of the study window of the Braddock-Fairchild apartment, high in the Cabrillo Building, Boysie Oakes thought that at any minute a huge, freckled Doris Day face would be superimposed on the Vistavision panorama.

The contrast between the view and the study interior was depressing. Commander Braddock-Fairchild, RN, was a man of habit. The room might have been the captain's cabin aboard one of Her Majesty's men-o-war. There was no colour here—not even in the bookcase, with its dull regimental leather bindings, covering half of one wall. The eye took in only the functional quality of the furnishings—heavy oak desk, solid leather armchair, wooden pipe-rack. The pictures—black and white photographs; some well-faded—told the familiar story of a naval officer: Braddock-Fairchild at Dartmouth, as a Midshipman, a Sub-Lieutenant, and so up the ladder. There were ships galore, shipmates aplenty: the only relief lying in a small framed photograph of the pleasurable Priscilla, standing at an exact angle on the Commander's desk.

Boysie had telephoned North Island Naval Base as soon as the trio got to their rooms. The Commander had been somewhat short, ordering Boysie to (his exact words) "Wait upon me in my apartment at six"—the heavy brow clouding darkly when Boysie arrived a good ten minutes late—after cautioning both Vladimir and Chicory to stay in their rooms, on the motel's upper deck, until his return.

Braddock-Fairchild listened silently—apart from loud sucking on a reeking pipe—and with total concentration, while Boysie told his story. There was a full minute's pause after he stopped speaking.

"Been expecting you for the last two days." There was no doubt that here was an officer and a gentleman—one of each. "Crossed me mind something might've gone wrong. Knew about your spot of bother in New York, of course. Had the local police up here asking questions of me daughter. Someone taking her name in vain, eh?"

"I rather gathered that, sir."

"Hurumph. Met her on the ship coming over, didn't you?"

"Yes. Is she well?"

"Probably see for yerself on your way out. Having a bath when you arrived. Can't understand these flibberty-gibbets. Suppose she's all right. Never eats anything; thin as a rake; goes around half naked. Wouldn't have done in my day. Still, her business. Whole country seems to have gone down since the war—tone of the place. Change and decay. Change and decay. Discipline, Oakes. That's what they need. Discipline."

"Yes, sir."

"Good. Now, you've got the Russian fellow at the motel with you? And the girl. She'll have to go back to New York, of course. I'll see that the Russian's taken care of. Your job's to be present at the trials on Monday. Personally, can't see how anything can go wrong. Americans look a slap-happy lot, but their security's first class. Couldn't get near that submarine if you were invisible—unless you were on the screened list or a crew member. Still, I'll have a word with their security boys. They'll check the net, seal up any chinks. Nothing more for you to worry about there, Oakes. Stay in the motel tonight. Have a car for you first thing in the morning—say 08.00 hours —bring you down to the wardroom at North Island. You'll be staying there, with the other observers, till the trials have finished. Briefin' begins 10.30—take most of the day. *Playboy's* scheduled to sail 09.00 on Monday. Any questions?"

"Will you be coming for the ride, sir?"

"If you mean, will I be sailing on *Playboy*, yes. I'm observing for the Royal Navy. Nothing else?"

"I don't think so."

"Good. Now, I want your room numbers at the motel. Just to make sure we collect the right people at the right times. Russian's in . . .?"

"29. I'm room 30, and Miss Triplehouse is in 31."

"Right." Braddock-Fairchild made a note on the pad at his elbow. "Get something to eat, then back to the motel. Keep in your rooms. See you in the morning; have to get on to the Base security boys now. Look's as if a good night's sleep wouldn't do you any harm. Find your own way out? Give me daughter a shout. Glad to see you."

Perplexed at the curt dismissal, Boysie went blinking through the door into the hallway of the apartment. Commander Braddock-Fairchild, RN, sat looking at the scribbled notes on the pad in front of him. He reached forward and picked up the telephone. The Commander's face betrayed none of the concern which niggled deep in the core of his well-ordered brain.

Boysie did not have to shout for Priscilla. She was leaning with her back against the wall facing the Commander's door; a slender goddess; jet hair hanging smooth to her shoulders; the firm body splendidly arranged under a cloud of white chiffon. From the room behind her the radio was playing something cool and swinging—it sounded like Brubeck's *Blue Rondo a la Turk*. In her right hand, Priscilla grasped a queen-sized frosted daquiri; her left stretched towards Boysie, offering him an equally large Courvoisier.

"Darling Boysie." The lips had that full, moist look. "I simply shrieked with joy when Daddy told me you were coming."

"Hallo," said Boysie.

She moved closer. "Kiss me and have a drink."

Boysie leaned forward and they touched lips. Hormones began doing the bossa nova.

"That's my boy." Priscilla handed over the drink. "How about taking a starving girl out to dinner?"

"Adore to but I've got no loose cash about me," said Boysie sipping his Courvoisier and giving her a look which the Lord Chamberlain and the Hayes Office would have ripped out without a second thought.

"I've got enough for both of us." Priscilla rubbed her back against the wall in a lazy arching movement.

"That's my girl." Boysie took the rest of his drink in one, and they closed like a pair of wrestlers.

San Diego's plushiest caravanserai, the *El Cortez Hotel*, sports a glass elevator which, to be different, ascends the high white building on the *outside*—pushed skywards on a single, shining steel shaft. As the ground dropped away, Boysie, never at his best where heights were concerned, swallowed hard and allowed his mouth to set in a sickly smile (praying that nothing would go wrong).

"Got stuck up here for fifteen minutes the other morning," said the wretchedly cheerful blonde attendant in reply to Priscilla's question about safety. After what seemed like a small piece of eternity, they stepped into the "Skyroom"—soft carpets, acres of glass, piped music and a platoon of padding waiters. Priscilla insisted that they begin the evening by toasting this fortuitous reunion in champagne: a decision which led to the only disturbance in an otherwise memorably voluptuous night. A waiter, fumbling the *Dom Perignon* '53, allowed the cork to make a premature escape—the resultant report cracking sharply on the eardrums of the dozen or so couples at that moment gorging themselves on the "Skyroom's" four starred provender. Boysie, whose nerves had just reached a state of comfortable complacency, wheeled from the table, dropping on one knee in the classic John Wayne-behind-a-boulder position—the big Stechkin in his right hand pointing unerringly at the wine waiter's portly stomach. A woman screamed. A retired Army major disappeared under the table, and a well-known Hollywood designer fainted away. Boysie went crimson and tried to hide the gun behind his back as he got to his feet making vague flapping gestures with his free hand. Priscilla giggled, spluttering into a dainty handkerchief.

"We do not encourage gunplay in this establishment, sir," said the head waiter pompously.

"Only a little joke. Toy pistol really." Boysie continued to flap his hand like a penguin.

Order was eventually restored. They were not asked to leave —Priscilla was known—but it was noticeable that departing diners made a careful detour to avoid passing the table where Boysie and Priscilla dined luxuriously on Oysters Kirkpatrick, Calf's Sweetbreads sauted in Bordelaise with Longbranch potatoes, and Strawberries Romanoff.

From the "Skyroom" they drove, in Priscilla's silver-grey Lancia 2800, out to the *Bali Hai* at the tip of man-made Shelter Island which projects from the north side of San Diego Bay. There, sitting on the stone terrace watching the moon spear its long phosphorescent reflection across the bay, and listening to the seductive schmaltz of Arthur Lyman, they drank what appeared to be footbaths of *Missionary's Downfall*—a pernicious blend of fresh lime, pineapple juice, fassionala and Martinique rhum negrite. An hour later, the Lancia sped them up to Point Loma where they discovered that, in spite of the more obvious spacial difficulties, it is quite possible in that make of automobile. It was almost one in the morning when Priscilla returned Boysie to the Sleepy Bear motel.

"And where do you think you've been?" Chicory's voice was audibly unpleasant. Boysie had been in the act of putting his key into the lock of room number 30, when her door swung open. Boysie smiled stupidly.

"What cheer, Chicky dear, I say, you look rather lovable in that get-up." Chicory's desirable flesh was covered only by a thin blue toga-style nightdress.

"The hell with my get-up, you louse. We've been waiting for you all night. Vladimir and I dined on . . . Guess what? . . . Stinkin' hamburgers, coffee, and half-a-bottle of Bourbon. I happened to have the Bourbon; Vladimir got the other stuff down at the Coffee Shop." Even Boysie, surrounded by the warm glow of *Missionary's Downfall* and post sexual self-confidence, could see that she was not exactly pleased to see him. He opened his mouth, but she was away again:

"And what's more, I've been waiting for *you*. I was in a state for you, Boysie. Then you turn up with . . . with . . ."

"Oh, I'm sorry. Hang on a minute. Chicory, and I'll come in to you . . ."

"Like hell you will. Vladimir's been trying to make me all night. Well, if I can't sleep, I'll go in to him. I never want to see you again, let alone sleep with you. You . . . you can go back to that . . . that anaconda who was twined all round you in the travelling brothel you arrived in. I saw you, Oakes . . . from my window I saw you . . . You're a two-timing lousy rat." And with that, Chicory Triplehouse slammed her door in his face.

Boysie's mind flipped. Pride would never allow him—even at this late hour, half stoned and eminently satisfied—to lose Chicory to Vladimir Solev. At a finger-snap he was into his room and across to the telephone. He asked for number 29. There was a lengthy pause before Vladimir's sleepy voice answered.

"Vladimir," said Boysie in a long-drawn coaxing tone.

"Who . . . Whosat?"

"Boysie. Look, Vladimir old chap, sorry to wake you up and all that, but I want to take a little safety precaution . . ."

"Whatsamatter?" Vladimir's nerves were showing.

"Haven't got time to explain now, but there's nothing for you to worry about . . ."

"You sure?" Very uncertain.

"Absolutely. Just want to play it safe. No panic, but I think it would be a good idea if we changed rooms."

"Why?"

"There isn't time to explain. Honestly. You've just got to trust me."

"All right, if you say so, Boysie. Change rooms. Now?"

"This minute."

"OK. Let me find some clothes."

"No time for that. Come as you are. Don't turn on any lights.

105

I'll meet you at the door go straight into your room. You come straight to mine, lock the door and get into bed. Don't talk and don't make any noise. OK?"

"OK. Oh, Boysie?"

"Yes?"

"I've remembered one thing."

"Yes."

"Gorilka told me the name of the operation—the code name for the operation."

"Well."

"It's Understrike—*Operation Understrike*'"

"Understrike, Schmunderstrike. That's a valuable bit of information, isn't it?" said Boysie sarcastically. "How do you think that's going to help?"

"Well, I just thought. . . ."

"All right. Thanks, Vladimir. Now get cracking, there's a good lad."

"I'm on my way."

Boysie smiled the smile of an irresponsible practical joker—the *Missionary's Downfall* still keeping him at bubbling point. Life was just a glorious game and the alarms and excursions of normality merely myths. In this warped, alcoholically-induced state he was even pleased to see that Vladimir's face wore the marks of fear, as the Russian tip-toed between the rooms modestly clutching a towel round his middle. Boysie stifled the desire to break into hysterical cackling mirth. The exchange was finally concluded, and within minutes of reaching Vladimir's room, Boysie had his clothes off and was in bed—naked and unashamed. Fifteen minutes later there was a soft, steady tapping at the door.

The night's events had told heavily on Boysie's stamina, and the noise jerked him back from the first stage of sleep. He blinked, shook his head, and remembered the little jape. Getting out of bed, he plodded across to the door.

"Who's there" His brain cloudy, he concentrated hard in an attempt to will his flagging senses into a more acute state of readiness.

"Me, Chicory. Let me in."

Boysie opened the door and Chicory nipped over the threshold—still dressed only in the blue bit of nothing.

"What do you want?" closing the door and sliding the chain into place.

"That's a stupid question after what happened earlier. I said I'd think about it. Well, here I am." She spread out her arms in the acknowledged stance of surrender: palms about eighteen inches from the thighs.

"You mean?" Boysie could see her quite clearly in the half-light. She nodded. He was close to her now, one hand around her waist, the other moving up to cup a nylon-shielded breast.

"I knew you'd come," he said softly. He was getting a body reaction now—lethargic maybe, but better than nothing.

"Did you, Vladimir?"

"Of course. Saw it in your eyes," said Boysie, butterflying it with his eyelids down her left cheek. Then maliciously, "Boysie back yet?"

"Don't talk about him, Vladimir. Just us. For a little while, just us."

How two-faced can a woman get? Boysie asked himself. She was pulling him gently towards the bed.

"Not so fast. I only just woke up."

"Come on. Please. For me." In the gloom, Boysie saw her hands move to the tiny bows—first at her shoulder and then the hip—which kept the film of toga in place. A slither and the nightdress dropped to the floor. Then they were between the sheets. Close. Rapturous.

Half an hour later, as the endearments and caresses were becoming sluggish, Boysie murmured, "Chicory, you are a real whizz . . ."

"Thank you, baby, you're a bang. Whizz-bang!"

Silence.

"Tell me . . .?"

"Yes?"

"How am I? . . . Compared to . . . to Boysie?"

"You don't want to talk about that."

"Please. I'd like to know." A kiss to the nose, and then just off-centre of the lips.

"You're both . . . Well, you're both very, *very* much alike. Quite 'strordinary," commented Chicory contentedly.

"Really?" Boysie was floating, but still in control and enjoying the joke.

"To be honest," Chicory was murmuring to herself as though under an anaesthetic, "he's probably a bit more vigorous than you. But what's an ounce or two of vigour between friends. What you lack in vigour you make up in subtlety, Vladimir."

Silence again.

"Vladimir?" A slow change in the contours of the thin sheet which covered them.

"Yes."

"Tell me about Russia."

"In the morning," said Boysie, aware of the danger inherent in this line of conversation, but too tired to do anything about it.

"I want to hear about Russia now."

"Very big, Russia."

"That's China. Noël Coward said it was China. Very big, China. That's what Noël Coward said."

"Well . . . Russia's very big."

"So's China . . ."

Chicory snuggled into the crook of Boysie's arm, and together they sank into a sleep, smooth and unruffled by dreams —oblivious to the fact that, only a few miles away, Dr Vassily Georg Gorilka, Khavichev's field commander for *Operation Understrike*, was holding a conference.

"THERE HAVE been set-backs. This must be admitted: I have myself made one bad error of judgment. Two of our assault operatives from the East coast have lost their lives—a small thing. I escaped—a big thing. But—and this is of great importance to your morale and our confidence in the ultimate success of this mission—nothing has so far happened that can in any way upset our plans for the final stage of this operation."

Gorilka looked down the table into five pairs of eyes. He could see respect glinting from all ten pupils. It gave him a magnificent sense of power. *Understrike* was the biggest job ever entrusted to him, and he was ruthlessly determined to make it the climax of his career. The men with him were also top operatives. He could trust them. Gorilka laid his paunchy hands over a blubbery stomach and continued:

"On the face of it, one of our comrades seems to have defected to the West. Or should I say defaecated to the West?" Gorilka enjoyed a joke. Khavichev was always telling people what a witty man Gorilka was. "But, my friends, our apostate knows nothing, nor is he in a position to give anything away. I show no concern for him because I am able to call him to heel at any moment I wish." The white, rubbery face screwed into a smile. "In fact, the two large gentlemen who arrived here with me tonight, are, at this moment, paving the way for our turncoat's return to our side of the street. Now, gentlemen, to the final arrangements . . ."

The conference lasted until the small hours.

JAMES GEORGE MOSTYN arrived by the Polar Route—the Boeing 707 sliding into San Francisco before dawn. Mostyn was a man of quite incredible single-mindedness—to the extent that some believed he had a predilection to *idées fixes*. Once the journey to America had begun, Mostyn's whole being centred on the big question mark which seemed to strangle Boysie and the *Playboy* firing trials. He started by trying to make a logical appreciation of the situation. From the scant evidence at his disposal, he knew that Boysie had gone missing—after abortive attempts both to kidnap and murder him—that the *Playboy-Trepholite* tests were of major importance to Western defence; that Boysie had been travelling to attend those tests; ergo, his disappearance did not bode well for the safety and security of either *Playboy* or its playmate *Trepholite*. Mostyn's intuition rarely let him down—especially where Boysie was concerned. The equation always came out the same: $B + P + T = C$ (Boysie + *Playboy* + *Trepholite* = Calamity).

As he sat in the San Francisco Terminal, sipping lukewarm coffee and waiting for the San Diego plane, Mostyn's sixth sense rippled like the muscles on a Mister Universe contestant. What, he wondered, were the opposition about? They could not mean to sabotage the submarine—that would be sheer foolhardiness. Surely they did not plan to pinch it? No, this was something far more perverse—and dangerous. Mostyn could feel it, as a countryman feels the approach of rain. But what? As he waited, Mostyn continued to research into the possibilities. Somewhere, he knew, there was a clue; a link; a missing factor.

FROM WAY back, Boysie was recalling a passage of Holy Scripture: *The Lamentations of the Prophet Jeremiah*, he thought. He was pretty certain it was from the *Book of Lamentations*. He could remember 'Old Noddler'—as the choirboys used to call the vicar so many summers ago in the Berkshire village church—reading at the great brass lectern. How they used to snigger, surpliced and hiding behind hymn books. Boysie was not sniggering now. "My bowels are troubled: my liver is poured out," he quoted silently, sitting in the cubicle bathroom of number 29. *Missionary's Downfall* had an extraordinary purgative effect. Boysie was not even able to wallow in retrospective pleasure about Chicory—who still lay deep in the arms of Morpheus, on Vladimir's bed.

Boysie knew it was simply a question of time before he would feel better. He had only got what Mostyn called "a touch of the scalds". With a head several sizes too large for him, Boysie closed one eye to focus more clearly on the dial of his wrist-watch. Seven-fifteen. Something was happening at eight. He made a tentative probe into the events of the previous evening, finally remembering that Braddock-Fairchild was sending a car to collect him at eight. Better shave. By this time he found that he had started to dress in Vladimir's clothes, laid neatly on a chair—as opposed to his own, lying in an untidy heap, and partly pushed under the bed.

"Oh what the hell," said Boysie. It was too late to bother

now. Go and shave. He moved gingerly back into the bathroom, then recollected that his own shaving kit was in the room
occupied by Vladimir. Chicory was still spark-out as he once
more crossed the room and made his way to number 30.

"Damn fool, Vladimir!" he muttered when the door opened
first time. "Idiot forgot to lock it."

Vladimir was also well away in Nodsville: the sheets pulled
right over his head, only a tiny lock of hair showing on the
pillow. Through the hectic shimmering mess which seemed to
be the inside of his skull, and appeared to be joined directly to
a similar réchauffé that was his stomach, Boysie considered the
situation. His joke with Chicory, such an hilariously nimble bit
of by-play in the early hours, now seemed stale. Chicory would
be livid. Best get washed, shaved and out to the Base without
waking either of them. They would find out soon enough.
Quietly he locked the bathroom door and, with hands which
resembled the wings of an anxious dragonfly, began his ablutions.

Twenty minutes later, much refreshed, Boysie donned
Vladimir's poloneck sweater, decided that it was too hot for
the climate, took it off and went into the bedroom to root among
his clothes for something more suitable. He chose the grey
cotton drifter shirt (with cream collar and two-button placket
front) which he had been dying to wear ever since getting on
to the ship at Southampton. He also gathered together, the small
pile of personal belongings—extra shirt (a cool blue creation by
Ambassadeur of Paris), the one remaining clean pair of pyjamas,
spare underwear and Onyx travel kit—needed for the night stop
at North Island Naval Base. Stuffing the soft gear into a flat Cunard shoulder bag, bought on the boat and so far unused, Boysie
prepared to go down and wait for the car in the parking lot.
His head and vitals still quavered, but something else had been
added to the general discomfort: a prickling, tingling sensation
up the short hairs at the back of his neck. Boysie looked round
the room. There was nothing out of place, yet he continued to
sense abnormality. Perhaps the silence was giving him the
jitters? The silence. Something was wrong. It was too quiet.

Vladimir! The lump lay very still under the sheet. Boysie could hear his own heart punching a heavy pulse. He took a couple of steps towards the bed. There was no movement, not even the rise and fall of breathing. He was trembling now, and the pulse rate—deafening in his ears—had become uncomfortably rapid. He wanted to get out, but conscience, and that odd magnetic pull towards the macabre, drew him closer to the bed. With thumb and forefinger of his right hand, Boysie slowly lifted the sheet.

There had been no struggle: a comparatively clean kill. Vladimir would have felt nothing: known nothing. He lay on his face with his head turned left, as though still in sleep—the only visible traces of violence being a blackened area about the size of a half-crown, behind the ear. It was the job of a professional. The assassin had come quietly in the night, skilfully forced the lock, walked up to the bed, held a small calibre weapon close to Vladimir's head (there must have been a silencer) and pulled the trigger. Boysie's shock reaction was fascination by the fact that there was little blood. Strangely, this amazed him. Vladimir's left hand was clenched tight, clutching at the pillow—an involuntary grab that must have been his only movement at the sudden crisis of death.

Boysie stood looking down at Vladimir's corpse, experiencing, not the usual nausea which overtook him in proximity to death, but a terrible empty well of sadness and grief. Then he realised that he was looking at himself. It was *his* body, the shell of *his* being, that lay among the crushed bedclothes: *his* head burst open by a .25 bullet from nowhere. The familiar swell of disgust frothed in his stomach, followed by a quick second wave as the full impact punched home. The bullet had been meant for *him*. If he had not changed rooms last night, it would be *him* on the bed, trussed by the bands of rigor mortis. First Joe Siedler. Now Vladimir Solev. The room reeled, and Boysie stumbled to the door for air. Stupidly, he saw that he was still hanging on to the Cunard bag and travel kit. Leaning against the balcony rail, taking long breaths of warm air through his nostrils, trying to steady his swimming head, Boysie heard a movement behind him. Chicory was standing in the doorway of number 29.

"Hi, Vladimir. Hey, you don't look so hot this morning."

Boysie's mouth was dry.

"Boysie about yet?" asked Chicory starting towards the adjoining room.

Boysie moved forward, his hands raised as though trying to push back an unseen obstruction. "Don't . . . Don't go in . . ." His voice sounded thin. Chicory continued to move, perplexed. "Don't go in!" He tried to shout, but could get no volume. "He's dead, Chicory. Dead . . ."

"But . . ." Chicory's face seemed to shrink, grey under the tan. Boysie was in front of her, barring the way. Gently he turned her round, pushing her back into the room where they had spent the night.

"He's dead. They shot him. The bastards shot him." Was all he could say. It sounded matter-of-fact: cold. Chicory gave a tiny moan and tottered on to the bed: the unbelievable truth not fully penetrating her mind. Boysie dimly realised that she still thought *he* was Vladimir. As far as she was concerned, he had brought her the news of his own death. He blundered around his mind trying to find the right words. Then the telephone began to burr its insistent warning.

Boysie jumped to a momentary heart-flutter, then automatically picked up the receiver.

"Yes?"

"Kharasho li vy spahli tovarich Solev?"

Confused as he was, Boysie recognised Russian and Solev's name. The pause grew, so he plunged in with the one word he knew:

"Da."

"Ah! Good! In English now I think." Unmistakably, the voice at the other end belonged to Gorilka. Boysie wanted to shout into the mouthpiece, to scream obscenities and fling abuse down the wires at the white spongy creep. Gorilka was still speaking.

"That is my old comrade, Vladimir Solev, isn't it?"

The minute fragment of Boysie's mind that still retained some contact with life, buzzed a cautionary signal: take care; don't give it away.

"Mmm." He made a vaguely affirmative noise.

"Vladimir, have you been to see your friend, Mr Boysie Oakes, this morning?"

"Yes." Disenchanted.

"Then you will know that we have caught up with him. We have a long arm, Vladimir. Nemesis always overtakes enemies of the people. You are not essential, but it would be better if you came back to us. Do you hear me?"

"Yes, I hear."

"You have been very foolish, but I can understand that you may have been under some unusual pressures."

I'd like to put you under some unusual pressures, Boysie thought. There was a wispy crackle of static on the line. Boysie remained silent. When Gorilka spoke again, the smoothness was gone; the voice sabre-sharp.

"Vladimir, if you do not do as I say, you will follow Mr Oakes. I would also advise you to think of your brother in Minsk, and your sister with her charming family in Odessa, perhaps also your old uncle who has that nice house near Rostov—your uncle Ivan. I can promise you, Vladimir, that if you do not follow my instructions, if you deviate a fraction from my orders, the whole Solev family will be as if they never were. That I vow. Do well and we might even be able to forget about your indiscretion."

Come home, all is forgiven, love Mother, thought Boysie. There'll always be a lamp in the window for our wandering boy. Christ, they really had old Vladimir by the short and curlies. What would Vladimir have done? More to the point, what should Boysie do? There was only one way. As far as the opposition was concerned he was Vladimir. He would have to remain Vladimir. Apart from anything else, it was the only way he could save his skin. These boys had bungled things a bit, but they would get him in the end.

"What do you want me . . ."

"To do? That's a good boy, Vladimir. Listen carefully. At any moment, a car will be arriving at your motel to carry Mr Oakes to North Island Naval Base. You will now become Boysie Oakes, just as we planned. You will impersonate the Englishman as you were trained to impersonate him. You will take his place at the firing trials. You will be under the command of our operative who is already on the Base. He will make himself known to you and pass on the detailed instructions. You will assist him throughout."

"Very good. I will do as you say." Boysie could hear Chicory still moaning on the bed behind him.

"And don't forget." Gorilka was smooth again. "Our people are everywhere. One slip on your part and the Solev family will ... But I am sure you understand ... Boysie. Take care, we are watching you."

The line went dead.

Leaving Chicory, Boysie hurried into room 30. He kept his eyes from the thing on the bed. On the table, only a few inches away from the clutching dead hand, lay Vladimir's Makarov pistol. Boysie slipped out the magazine and checked that it was fully loaded with its eight 9mm cartridges. Ramming the magazine back into the butt recess, he cocked the weapon, clicked on the safety catch and slid the pistol into the pocket of his slacks. It would be less conspicuous than the big Stechkin.

The lock had been only slightly damaged by the intruder. Hanging the little cardboard *Do Not Disturb* sign on the outer handle, Boysie left the room, closing the door behind him.

"Vladimir ... Please, can I see him?" Chicory, for all her moaning, had not shed a tear. That would come later, thought Boysie. She sat on the bed looking white and tired. "No, Chicory. I mean it, no." There was no time to explain: no time to tell her. "I don't want you to go near that room." He was talking quickly edging for the door. "Pack, pay your bill and get out of here. Get the first flight to New York. Just get away. You've got money?"

She nodded.

"Call your people, your department, the people who sent you—call Max as soon as you arrive."

The blast of an automobile horn from the parking lot below.

"Will you do that, Chicory? Will you do as I say?"

"Can't I come with you? I'm frightened."

"Do you think I'm not? It's better to split up. Run."

"All right. But I'd like to see . . ."

"I've locked the door," he lied. "Don't try to get in."

The horn again. Impatient.

"Look, I have to go. You'll be all right."

"Won't I see you again?"

"Of course. Someone'll be in touch. But we've got to make it on our own now. Good luck, Chicory."

Boysie did not stop to be chivalrous. He did not even stop to kiss her. Some of Boysie's professional training stuck hard. He knew that he must go on: get out on the limb, and hope. In his mind he was spinning the biggest prayer wheel ever. Every nerve-end and organ seemed to be riddled with anxiety, but his only chance lay within the barbed wire fences of North Island Naval Base.

It was not until he was in the US Navy Chevriolet that he really began to think about the next move.

"Gotta hurry," said the white-uniformed sailor driver, handing Boysie a small official card which was his passport to the Base: his credentials. "Base is sealed off after 09.00. Nobody, authorised or unauthorised, is gonna be able to get in or out. Nobody."

As the car hummed through the hot streets, it struck Boysie that he could do nothing but play at being a double agent. The opposition—he knew from Gorilka—had at least one operative planted inside the Base: probably even taking an active part in the *Playboy-Trepholite* trials. To most people, Boysie would be Brian Oakes, British Special Security observer. But to one, maybe two, or even three men, he would be Vladimir Solev, there to assist in *Operation Understrike*—whatever that may be. Boysie dared not open his thumping heart to anybody. There was nobody he could trust. This, he argued to himself, was one of the reasons for leaving Chicory so quickly.

"It's all very difficult," he said to himself, wrapped in acute depression.

The hangover, the ugliness, the shock of death, and the decisive call to action had, until now, sublimated the more noisy facets of Boysie's shrieking fear. Alone, in the back of the car, the trembling and cold sweat of continual apprehension slushed over him. Outside the car, the world was quiet and content. The great American way of life rolled smoothly by on plastic runners. The Moms were raiding the supermarkets and arguing over the way to keep from getting pregnant again, or how to avoid domestic maladjustment within the family unit; the Pops were in their offices slaving away for the status symbol of an ulcer or a nervous breakdown; the teenagers were living it up on 7-*Up*, kookie and kinky, shaking to the Blue Beat or Country and Western; the kids were munching Hershey bars and getting sick off soda pop; the old timers were amazed at the speed of life in the space age. Crooks were crooking; junkies were junking; lovers were loving; rapists were raping; TV stars were showing their teeth; regular guys were being outwardly regular, while inwardly they thought about seducing their neighbour's wives or—if they had passed middle age—their neighbour's daughters. People were just going about their quite everyday tasks—taking sleeping pills and tranquillisers, going to bed with their sisters, getting hopped up, killing people, having babies out of wedlock, lying, cheating, stealing. God was in orbit: all was well in the land of the free: Ma's apple pie tasted great. And Boysie Oakes was isolated, right slap bang centre in a bullseye which marked the middle of a plot angled to add a little chaos to democracy. Boysie Oakes was not happy. He longed for a change of scene: a new job even.

The car pulled up at an intersection, stopped by traffic lights, Boysie had that unnerving feeling that someone was watching him. Another car had drawn level with them—a shining black 300SE limousine. At the wheel sat a pugilistic man with a small scar below his right eye. Boysie looked into the back of the car. The tiny eyes of Dr Vassily Georg Gorilka stared back at him, expressionless. Gorilka inclined his head towards Boysie, after the manner of royalty. The lights changed and the two cars leaped forward. At the next cross roads the 300SE turned right. The US Navy Chevrolet went straight on, carrying Boysie Oakes towards North Island Base.

MOSTYN HAD the right mentality for security work—sneaky. He had arrived in San Diego incognito: Unheralded and as anonymous as the father of an artificially inseminated child. In spite of his lack of immediate credentials, one telephone call to North Island Base had produced the information that the British Security officer called Oakes had arrived and was staying at the Sleepy Bear motel. That was a bit easy, thought Mostyn, should have their guts for that: chivvy the darlings; could have given Boysie's address to any Tom, Dick or Boris—not good enough (he smiled at the bad pun). So Boysie was here in San Diego. That was a relief. But what had Boysie been doing en route? If the Chief was right, and their lad had been giving way to concupiscence . . .! Mostyn burned at the very idea. I will have his genitals for breakfast—he threatened silently—with tomatoes. As the cab rattled him towards the Sleepy Bear motel, Mostyn allowed himself the luxury of a short daydream concerning Boysie in excruciating agony.

Mostyn arrived at the motel just before nine-fifteen. The morning was warm and clear: the palm fronds and bougain-villaea trembling a little to the mild breeze.

"Either 29 or 30 depending which one ya want," said the manager in answer to Mostyn's polite request for Boysie's room number. This was confusing, but Mostyn always found himself being confused in the United States.

"The dame just checked out—'bout ten minutes ago," added the manager.

So Boysie *had* been leching it across the States. From the start, Mostyn had not liked the sound of FEMALE ESCORT mentioned in the cables. By the time he reached room number 30, the Second-in-Command of British Special Security was deep in a mood of icy sadism. The *Do Not Disturb* sign swung daintily from the handle.

"I'll do not disturb him," murmured Mostyn rapping hard on the door. "Come along, old boy. I know you're in there. Surprise. See who's come all the way from London on the wild goose run!" He knocked again, the lock slipped and the door swung open. Mostyn blinked twice, and made it to the bed in a single bound. The sneer turned to a look of revulsion.

"God!" he breathed, staring down at the body of Vladimir Solev. "What have they done to you, old boy? Poor old Boysie, what have they done to you?"

VI – UNDER . . .

"CLASS-CONSCIOUS heap of capitalists," muttered Boysie surveying his fellow observers with acid animosity. From the moment Commander Braddock-Fairchild took him into the wardroom, where they were gathered for coffee before the day's work, Boysie felt out of his depth—not the happiest way to begin a submarine trip under the Pacific Ocean. On top of the other anxieties, Boysie was getting an inferiority kick.

The special representatives had been chosen from Navy, Army, Air Force and Security services of both Great Britain and the United States; and Boysie instantly recognised the British Army Major and the Air Force Wing-Commander as Eton-Oxford embassy-attaché-type wet snots.

"Don't see why we're here at all," the Major drawled, sleek and polished next to Boysie in his casuals. "Just to sit in a damned submarine. American flamboyancy that's all it is. What sort of report we goin' to be able to write, eh? Won't even see the missile go up. Eh, Tiger?"

"Typical," was all that Tiger—the Wing-Commander—could contribute.

Braddock-Fairchild bumbled (stupid old duffer, thought Boysie) and introduced the Americans. Their security man—a diminutive Texan called Rondinelli—said "Hi!"; the Naval, Army and Air Force officers just stared, nodded and went back to their private argument about the last Army/Navy game. At the far side of the room, about thirty US Navy Officers—who were to watch the trials the easy way—on the monitors set up in the operations room, safe ashore—clustered together, making like a suburban cocktail party: all chat and teeth. Landlubbers, thought Boysie.

After standing with a fixed grin, and speaking to nobody for ten minutes, Boysie took his coffee into a corner and opened the leather folder presented to each of them on arrival. One thing was sure: the opposition had not planted their man among the eight special observers. They were all as obsolete as the halberd, was Boysie's ultimate decision.

The leather folder had 'Most Secret' embossed in the top right-hand corner. But its contents yielded little that security could classify as risky. First, a list of the official observers—Boysie's name misspelled as 'Oaks'. Seven pages of biographical details, capsuling the service careers of senior officers taking part in the exercise, a short history of submarine warfare, and a single sheet headed *Program for Official Special Observers: Playboy-Trepholite Firing Trials* completed the file. This final page was, to Boysie, the only useful thing in the whole load of bumph. It clearly stated the times of meals (not that we're likely to get any *cordon bleu* here, he thought), and gave an explicit picture of how they were expected to spend the next few hours. An introductory talk, by Admiral Charles Fullenhaft would be followed by Captain Gary O'Hara (Commanding *USS Playboy*) giving his briefing to the observers. In the afternoon they were to be taught safety drill, and at 17.00 all personnel—civilians, officers and enlisted men—taking part in the trials, had to be present for a final briefing. The eight observers, Boysie noted ruefully, were required—dressed, clean, sober and in their right, tiny, cotton-picking minds—at 05.30 on Monday morning ready for embarkation in *Playboy*.

The lecture room was small and uncomfortable. It reminded Boysie of school (there was that same chalky smell), and later of the interminable lectures he had endured—shuttled from training course to training course—during World War II. On the right of a raised dais stood an easel displaying a large-scale chart of San Diego Bay and a mighty hunk of the Pacific; on the left, a similar easel held a coloured sectional diagram of a submarine—presumably the famous *Playboy*.

"It is my pleasurable duty to welcome you here as official observers for these trials involving the most advanced sub aqua craft the world has yet seen—*USS Playboy*—and its particular missile, the *Trepholite*." The arid voice of Admiral Charles Fullenhaft growled soporifically in the mid-morning warmth.

Under his breath, Boysie muttered, "Here they are . . . Your friends and mine . . . Ladies and Gentlemen . . . a big hand for . . . Per-lay-boy . . . and Ter-repholite!"

"Before Captain O'Hara speaks to you," the Admiral looked set for a good half hour. "I would like to explain just why the United States Navy and the State Department deemed it desirable to have certain independent observers present on this historic occasion . . ."

The tensions of the past days were pressing in on Boysie. It only needed Admiral Fullenhaft's tranquillising pedantry to set the veils of sleep billowing round his mind. Twice he nodded forward. The third time found him off his chair, having to be helped up by the laconic Rondinelli. The Admiral's secretary, a lean hungry Lieutenant, pointedly opened the window.

The Admiral buzzed on, ". . . The submarine must move to live; while it is moving it is detectable. You are all aware of the increasing importance of sub aqua launching pads. Because of them, International Limits have no strategic significance. Our deployed nuclear submarine power is at once a silent strike force and a last ditch retaliatory unit . . ." Boysie decided to try out the game they used to play during sermons—when he was in the village choir. You listened for a word beginning with A, and B and so on until the end of the alphabet. XYZ were the difficult ones.

". . . Success in the nuclear war can only be achieved by the complete and immediate destruction of the enemy's powers of retaliation. Our *Polaris* submarines—operating for long periods below the ocean—are almost immune from surprise attack . . ." Up to F already.

"But, gentlemen," the Admiral was allowing his voice to slide into the grave funeral oration level. "We must not delude ourselves. In spite of this great country's advances in the relatively new field of nautical strategy and technocracy, we must face the fact that the USSR has, until now, remained steadily ahead of us—both numerically (with submarines afloat) and in strike power: you will all be conversant with the formation of Russia's new attacker fleet of sixty large, nuclear, missile-carrying submarines. But, with the *Playboy-Trepholite* complex in full production, we will now have the edge on any navy in the world." He paused, searching for applause. Getting none the Admiral gazed steadily at his notes and continued. Boysie had got to I.

"The balance of power lies in *Playboy*. She is the fastest, most manoeuvreable nuclear submarine yet devised by any nation. Equipped with the HK5 radar beam-bender, she is virtually undetectable. Her sole purpose is to operate as a silent, rapid, annihilative attack platform. She carries—and can launch from the submerged position—six *Trepholite* missles." Boysie was still listening out for J. "At first sight this may seem a small number compared to such craft as *George Washington*, designed to carry sixteen *Polaris* missiles." No. J.

"Now, gentlemen, obviously, even at this level, I cannot give you the full specifications of *Trepholite*. But I can assure you that it is the answer to our prayers. God is on our side gentlemen. Its accurate range, from the submerged craft, is in excess of 3000 miles, and its nuclear punch far exceeds the ICBM figures released last year. One *Trepholite* . . ." He sounded as though he was about to deliver an ultimatum, "can deliver the megadeath power of six *Polaris*. Sixteen *Polaris*, launched simultaneously, have a destructive power equal to that of all bombs detonated during World War II . . . So you can work it out for yourselves." Stuck on J. There's no justice, thought Boysie, and gave up the game. The Admiral was still talking.

"The greatest single factor in *Trepholite's* favour, as you will see, is its size. In relation to range, accuracy and power, this is a comparatively small missile—due to the phenomenally tiny *Dies Irae* warhead and the new X4F metallic compound developed by the Sandia Corporation . . ."

The size, range and power of the *Trepholite* meant little to Boysie. His mind could not encompass such things. To him, the *Trepholite* was simply a super shell which could be fired from under the sea, travel a long distance, and end up with a bloody great bang—killing a lot of people, maiming hundreds more, and spreading a deadly toxic sprinkle into the atmosphere. Yet even Boysie could see it was an important weapon. The faces around him all radiated the same resigned gloom.

Captain Gary O'Hara now took the stand—a very different can of fish from the Admiral. O'Hara was a compact, aggressive, fly-weight who came straight to the point.

"Gentlemen, my name's O'Hara and you will be under my command while you are on board *Playboy* tomorrow. Some of you may wonder why we have asked for observers actually on board. We want you aboard for two reasons. First, you will be able to make a more accurate evaluation of the *Trepholite's* mobility from the radar scanners and TV screens on *Playboy*. Second, we want you to see for yourselves the ease of firing this weapon—its basic simplicity. The only thing you will not see, is the strike power; but none of us'll see that until the balloon goes up anyway: perish the thought."

Boysie still fought drowsiness.

"As you've only got two naval officers with you, I'm going to avoid technicalities. This is *Playboy*." He pointed to the sectional cutaway plan. The submarine looked like a fat, strangely-bumped fish: the conning tower—set well to the rear—sprouting a pair of unlikely-looking fins, the forward deck rising to a streamlined bulge at the bows. It reminded Boysie of the Hammer-head sharks he had seen at the zoo with Elizabeth on his last leave. O'Hara went on.

"*Playboy* is powered by one pressurised water-cooled reactor. Geared turbines. Length 447 feet. Beam twenty-five feet. Six *Trepholite* missiles housed in the launching area forward." He indicated the bulge. "Though for the trials we will only be carrying two. Tomorrow you will enter the craft through the main forward hatch in the sail—that's what we used to call the conning tower. Now it's called the 'sail', sometimes the 'fair-weather'. You will spend the entire trip in this area . . ." His hand hovered over a section within the ship's hull, directly below the sail—the first of four decks which formed the living and working quarters. "In an operational craft this would be the Officers' Quarters, but for this exercise we have fitted it out as an Observation Platform. You will be seated—as comfortably as we can manage—against the hull: four on either side: and you'll watch the operation on two thirty-inch radar scanners and two TV screens which will give you pictures of the launching from the surface and the scenes at the strike areas. One of my officers will be present throughout, to keep you advised of progress and to point out anything of special, or technical, importance." O'Hara paused to take a long swig of water.

"The Control Deck—from which I command, and from which the missiles will be aimed and fired, is immediately forward of your Observation Platform." On the plan the Control Deck was outlined in blue. "You will be taken on board around 05.30 tomorrow. We sail at 09.00 and will submerge approximately two miles out from San Diego Bay. From there we go full speed for the launching area—roughly forty-five miles West of where we are sitting now. We begin the firing countdown around 13.30 and we're going to make two demonstration strikes. The first against a radio-controlled aircraft flying at 40,000 feet due West of us. The second on an obsolete cruiser —USS Fireman—anchored 200 miles due West. These shots, of course, don't demonstrate the true range of Trepholite." The Captain smiled and, Boysie observed, slyly transferred his hand from pocket to mouth.

"Captain O'Hara has a passion for ju-jubes," whispered Rondinelli.

O'Hara had quickly consumed the candy and was still talking at speed: "To some extent we're going to be cheating tomorrow as far as the aircraft shoot is concerned. The missile, in this case, will not be beamed on to its target from Playboy, but homed by the ICD Mk IV Homer fitted into the target aircraft."

O'Hara rolled down another diagram on the submarine easel and explained the workings of the ICD Mk IV Homer—an instrument not much bigger than a matchbox, capable of sending a pre-selected bleep over long ranges. A similar apparatus, in the nose of the missile, is set to corresponding bleep series, which it tracks until physical contact is made. The whole mystique of this instrument eluded Boysie, to whom electronics were anathema.

"The bleep settings will be checked and corrected from the Control Deck fifteen minutes before firing; but I intend to show you the firing procedure on the spot tomorrow," continued O'Hara. "Last, a word about safety. When we are fully operational, the Control Room and Officers' Quarters—your Observation Platform—are sealed off from each other and the three decks immediately below: that is, the crew's quarters, galley, electric space and store rooms. The only access to these decks is through the main hatch in the Control Room which, on this occasion, will be closed before we sail. The Control Deck bulkhead door—which is your link with me and my staff —is made fast from inside the Control Deck. Tomorrow I'm going to leave the Control Deck bulkhead door open until forty-five minutes before firing, so that you can see how we operate the craft underwater. It's a bit cramped, of course, so we'll have you up on the Control Deck in pairs. In the event of damage or accident, both the Control Deck and Officers' Quarters are fitted with two escape tubes. You may know that it is not normally the policy of the United States Navy to make provision for escape tubes in submarine design. We rely on the McCann Rescue Bell, which will be carried in our Depot ship—accompanying the surface craft at the firing point tomorrow. But, as this is a prototype vessel we have been experimenting with a form of escape tube that we consider an advance on both the British Davis method and the Twilltrunk escape hatch. You will be issued with P50 escape apparatus—there's a breathing mask which will take you up to the surface with very little discomfort. You'll be instructed on the use of the escape tubes and the P50 this afternoon."

This was something Boysie had not anticipated. He was almost always sick in aeroplanes. What if he discovered, too late, that he had an allergy to submarines? Some dreadful claustrophobic twitch which made him run berserk, claw at the bulkheads and scream to be taken to the surface. He became so absorbed in the possibilities of this new anxious terror, that he missed the final part of Captain O'Hara's briefing.

In the afternoon, a US Marine sergeant and two slick submariners put them through the safety drill; showed them how to slip on the frogman-like mask, step into the cramped gun barrel of the escape tube, check the hatch fastening, inflate the life-jacket, pull the red switch, watch the dial and wait until the pressure in the tube equalised with the external pressure before throwing the green lever which would shoot you from the submarine—sending the escapee flying to the surface like an Alka-Seltzer bubble. They also pointed out the terrible results of pulling the green lever too soon; and taught the observers how those still within the craft could re-set the tube for the next escape.

At five o'clock they assembled—with what seemed to be the entire manpower of the US Navy—in the huge briefing room. It was here that Boysie lost contact with the whole affair, becoming an innocent among the technocrats. Weather experts talked about pressures; navigation officers went away into little worlds of their own—bounded by minutes, degrees, latitudes, longitudes and drifts; charts were rolled and unrolled; people talked about Red Zones, Pink Zones and Green Zones. It just went on and on until Boysie was only conscious of the Numb Zone around his buttocks.

Boysie was still playing his waiting game, and nobody had even hinted that they were the opposition's man on North Island. But, as he stood outside the briefing room, trying to make up his mind about the direction of the wardroom, a grim, beautifully turned out US Navy officer tapped him on the shoulder.

"Mr Oakes?" He was an intense man with huge hands and a habit of wrinkling his nose before he spoke—as if every word wasn't using Amplex.

"Yes."

"British Special Security?"

"That's right."

"My name's Birdlip: Senior Intelligence Officer for this base. Sorry to trouble you, but we've had a nut in the brig all day says he's the Second-in-Command of your outfit."

Boysie's heart did a couple of tricks that would have pleased Joe Morello. Birdlip went on.

"I've been on to London, but they don't seem to know anything about him. Would you mind having a look. Checking for us? Just to make sure. Could be a Redland try-on because his passport and ID card look like they're OK. Personally, I think the guy needs mental treatment. Gave us a lot of trouble this morning."

They took Boysie to a bleak stone building near the main gate, and down a narrow passage, between regularly-spaced solid cell doors. Somewhere an off-white voice was singing "Just a wearyin' for you." At the end of the passage they stopped, and Birdlip indicated a peep-hole set in the door of the last cell. Boysie closed one eye and squinted. There, looking as though he would explode with rage, sat Mostyn—confined and solitary. Boysie's bowels leaped. He could not do with Mostyn at this stage. For all he knew, Birdlip might even be his opposition contact. Boysie was playing at being a double agent. Intuitively he knew Mostyn's advent would only mean trouble. For a moment he hesitated. Then, almost perversely—remembering all the times that Mostyn had caused him pain and embarrassment—he made up his mind. Mostyn would just have to sweat it out. "Never seen the fellow in my life," lied Boysie with a blank face.

MOSTYN HAD made it from room 30 to the road at a rate of knots.

"Taxi!" he yelled at a passing cab. Mostyn always cultivated the English-abroad technique when in the United States. It gave him a sense of one-upmanship and the locals seemed to like it.

"Where to, bud?"

"North Island Naval Base, and hurry." He was into the cab and bouncing around the rear seat as the driver performed a

U-turn with his foot down. Mostyn's one thought was to get to the Base and solicit for official help.

"You from England?" He had picked a talkative cab-driver.

"Yes." Mostyn was in no mood for the barber's shop routine. His mind had turned into a cold, ruthless spot. An operative under his command lay dead. He would like to know why? He wanted revenge: Mostyn was a devout eye-for-an-eye man.

"Thought ya was from England. London?"

"Yes."

"I gotta sister-in-law in London. Mabel Schwertzeobber. Ever hear of her?"

"I haven't had the pleasure."

"In the rag trade—clothing business. Meddlesome old bat. Wants ta come over ta visit next fall. It's my boy Hymie's *Bar Mitzva*, see. Big day in a boy's life. Well, we got family troubles. Nothin' worse than family troubles, Mack. Take my word for it. I know. Family troubles can really do for a man."

"I'm sure." Mostyn made the right noise.

"Sure. I know. I'm tellin' ya. Family troubles I got, mister, but right. This Mabel, she wants ta come for Hymie's *Bar Mitzva*. Well, my old lady, she hadda fight with her. Years back. They even forgot now what they wus fightin' about. She says, now, that Mabel ain't settin' a foot inside my door. You can choose, she says, it's either her'n me . . ."

Mostyn had ceased to hear. The cab-driver's domestic crisis flowed over him—an unavoidable irritation, like bees at a picnic. Mostyn was thinking about Boysie, *Playboy* and *Trepholite*.

At the main gate, he paid off the cab and walked over to the Marine guard, a tall smartie inflated with brief authority. Mostyn flashed his Special Security card.

"Colonel Mostyn. British Special Security. I must see your Commanding Officer immediately."

The guard rubbed one side of a very smooth jaw with the white truncheon which hung, sinister, from his wrist.

"No can do."

"I beg your pardon?"

"I said, no can do!"

Mostyn waited. The guard looked at him, his face set and suspicious.

"I must see your Commanding Officer. This is an emergency. Vital importance to your country's security."

"And I said, 'no can do'. President himself couldn't see the Old Man today. Base is closed tighter'n a badger's. Closed to everybody. But everybody."

"Look," said Mostyn, carefully enunciating, as a tourist explains cricket to a Bulgarian peasant. "I am the Second-in-Command of British Special Security—a post not without some weight . . ."

"Yea?" The guard left no doubt as to his disbelief. Under his breath, he said, "Bet ya never even seen that Christine babe. . . ."

"This is my identity card and this is my passport," still carefully enunciating. "If you cannot take me to your Commanding Officer at least have the good manners to call your immediate superior." Even in the rising heat, Mostyn felt cold. His tact hung precariously by a hair.

"You got trouble, Irwin?" A Marine sergeant was leaning round the guardroom door.

"Guess so, sergeant. Better get Lootenant Dooley down here." He gave Mostyn a nod. "Ya'd better come into the guardroom . . . sir." The 'sir' was added with a flavour of facetiousness.

Mostyn sat in the guardroom, for half an hour, while they located Lieutenant Dooley. No one spoke to him, though all who passed by looked him up and down as though viewing a freak at a fair. Dooley turned out to be what the Chief would have called "an officious young cub".

"I understand you have demanded entrance to this Base, sir," he said, solemnly.

"I . . ." began Mostyn controlling his ire with a supreme effort of will.

But Dooley blithely talked over him.

". . . Nobody is allowed entrance to this Base without a

permit issued by the State Department of the United States of America, counter-stamped by United States Naval Intelligence. I understand you have produced no such pass. In any case, this Base is closed to everybody today."

"Have you quite finished?" Mostyn gave him the glare treatment. Dooley nodded calmly, "Good. Then let me tell *you* something. My name is Mostyn. Colonel Mostyn. Colonel James George Mostyn. I am Second-in-Command of British Special Security. One of my operatives should be here. On this base. At this moment. Being briefed for the firing trials of your missile *Trepholite* from the submarine *Playboy*. That operative is not on this base because I have just found him lying dead, in bed, at the Sleepy Bear motel—room 30. His code designation is 'L'. His name is Oakes. Brian Ian Oakes. And these are my credentials." He held out his card and passport.

Dooley's expression did not alter. He took the documents from Mostyn and gave them a quick going over. This guy, he thought, was either big and for real, or right off his curly little nut.

"Guess you'd better wait a minute." Dooley had a hurried and stealthy conversation with one of the Marines, then disappeared into an inner office. The guard did not take his eyes from Mostyn. Afer five minutes Dooley returned.

"Our Senior Intelligence Officer will be down in a while. Would you like to step in here?" Mostyn followed him into the office—grey, airy and seemingly dust-proof. He was kept waiting for a further three quarters of an hour. By the time Dooley reappeared with the SIO, Mostyn had reached a state of internal seeth akin to Vesuvius at eruption minus two.

"Commander Birdlip," introduced Dooley. "Commander Birdlip, this is Colonel . . . Mostyn." He stressed the 'Colonel'.

"Colonel Mostyn," nodded Birdlip crisply. "You quite comfortable in that chair? Just relax, hunh?"

Mostyn boiled over.

"This is not the time for comfort or bloody relaxation. I have been sitting in jet-propelled aeroplanes for the last ten hours. I have come to your God-forsaken, pre-packed, hygienicallywrapped, mint-flavoured country because I thought one of my men was in trouble. This morning I arrived at this wretched watering place and found my man dead. I have reason to believe that his death is linked with the *Playboy-Trepholite* firing trials which, even you must know, are being held here. Will you bloody do something about it?"

"I don't think you need raise your voice. We are already doing something about it." Birdlip spoke like a nurse buttering a lid-flipped patient. "I have already checked on you. *A* Colonel Mostyn *is* Second-in-Command of British Special Security, but I'm afraid we have no signal from London intimating that we are to expect his arrival here. Therefore, sir, I must view you with suspicion—in spite of your documents, which Lieutenant Dooley tells me he has inspected."

Mostyn raised his eyes to heaven and counted ten as slowly as the burning temper would allow.

"Well, why, old boy," he said on a note of shimmering frostiness, "don't you call London for confirmation, and send somebody down to the Sleepy bloody Bear motel . . ."

"We are putting in a call to London now." Birdlip was the essence of good manners. "And a squad car is on its way to the Sleepy Bear."

Mostyn sighed. At last he was getting a little action.

It was early evening in London. In St Paul's Cathedral the Bishop of Scunthorpe was preaching on the text, "Jeshurun waxed fat, and kicked" (Deuteronomy XXXII: 15). It had been a warm day for a change. The Chicken Inns and coffee bars were crowded; Hyde Park was littered; there had been a protest in Trafalgar Square; in Bayswater a girl called Hazel Plunket had lost her virginity (together with approximately 200 other girls in the London area that day); there had been seven fatal accidents, and the Queen was spending Sunday at Windsor. Unknown to the Press and general public, in Number 10 Downing Street the Prime Minister was preparing to fly secretly to the United States for a meeting with the President. Precautions had been taken by the Department of Special

Security, who had labelled the trip *Topmeet*. Its classification was *Clandestine*.

Susan Boowright—on the switchboard at the Whitehall head-quarters of Special Security—took the incoming transatlantic call from San Diego, and passed it straight through to Lieu-tenant Peach, the day's Duty Officer. Peach covered the re-ceiver with his hand and spoke to the duty secretary, a sad willowy girl with a halitosis problem.

"Number Two isn't out of the country, is he?" asked the puzzled DO.

"Don't think so. Anything in the Movements File?"

"No. US Navy Base at San Diego say they've got a bloke there claiming to be Colonel Mostyn. Better call the Chief."

The Chief's private number did not reply. He was spending the week-end, with Mrs Chief, at a house party in Hampshire and had, characteristically, neglected to inform the DO of his whereabouts.

The DO rang Mostyn's private number. The phone burred in an empty flat.

"Sorry," said the DO to the caller far off in sunny San Diego, "I'm afraid I've no note of Colonel Mostyn's movements, but we're pretty certain he hasn't left the country. We'll call con-firmation as soon as possible."

He made a note on his preliminary report card: "19.00 hours, telephone link with North Island Base (Navy), San Diego, Cali-fornia, USA; regarding Colonel Mostyn's movements. Possible impersonation. Pending."

Mostyn had done as he was commanded, and left in a hurry. The Chief had promised to pass on his action to all sections of the Department. The Chief had done nothing. It would wait until Monday.

"I'VE GOT news for you." Birdlip replaced the telephone receiver and regarded Mostyn with steady severity. "One of my officers just called London. British Special Security say that as far as they know, their Colonel Mostyn is still in England."

"But . . ." Mostyn was raging. "But there must be . . . this is . . . this is ridiculous. Let me speak to them . . . call them again . . . I *am* Mostyn . . . Hang it, everyone knows *me* . . ."

"I think I should tell you something else . . ."

"This is quite outrageous . . . Heads will roll . . . What?"

"The Special Security man, Oakes, is already on the Base. I've rechecked his credentials. Everything tallies. He's Oakes all right. Photograph. Everything."

"Look, Hairlip . . ."

"Birdlip . . ."

". . . or whatever your damn name is. I saw the man dead I tell you. I'm not mad . . ." Again the telephone rang. Birdlip answered. The conversation was brief and monosyllabic. When it finished, Birdlip once more gave Mostyn the disparaging eye.

"That was Captain Boyle, San Diego City Police Department. There is no corpse in room 30 at the Sleepy Bear." Sulphurically: "The occupant checked out. Manager says he was a bit drunk and friends came for him. Bill paid in full. Now, buster, where did you get that passport and ID card? And where did you get the information about the *Playboy-Trepholite* firing trials?" Birdlip, Dooley and the two shining Marines seemed to close in on Mostyn.

Mostyn could not remember a time when he was more livid.

"Dive! dive! Dive!"

The urgent caw of the klaxon alarm.

"Angle of descent 25 degrees."

"25 degrees, sir."

"Check descent . . . Full pressure."

"Take her to one hundred fifty feet."

"One . . . Five . . . Zero feet."

"Check angle of descent."

The bulbous shape of *Playboy* disappeared smoothly under the calm blue water of the Pacific, leaving a white broil of foam which spread gurgling in great whirlpools, eddied, then finally settled leaving no trace.

On the Observation Deck, Boysie felt as fluttery as when

sitting in an aircraft on take-off. They had come aboard just before six—a small picket boat bouncing them over the Bay to the Depot ship, lying alongside the submarine, surrounded by a small flotilla of light craft ready to accompany her, on the surface, out to the firing area. The American Army Major had looked as though he was going to be sick. The British Army Major had been. Both seemed all right now.

The Observation Deck was larger than Boysie had anticipated: an area about twenty-four feet long, with a surprising amount of space to move between the central bank of radar scanners and TV monitors: the decor dark grey, lit by pinkish strip lighting. The observers sat in deep bucket seats bolted to the stanchions against the hull: four on either side: Americans to port, British to starboard—segregation to the end. Boysie, in the forward seat, next to Braddock-Fairchild, could see through the open bulkhead door on to the Control Deck where Captain O'Hara sat—in a comfortable swivel chair—facing the angled, switch and dial strewn desk which curved in a half-circle below a battery of apparatus. To the Captain's left sat the Navigation Officer. The Ballistics Officer (in charge of the *Trepholite* launching equipment) was on the right. Just inside the bulkhead, Boysie could glimpse the back of the Communications' Control Officer, a Lieutenant weighed heavy with the responsibility of maintaining contact with the world above them. On the far left was the Coxswain, hands held loosely on the polished wheel, no bigger than that of an automobile: sitting like the driver of some supersonic bus. Somewhere, out of sight, there was an Electronics Officer. The whole Central Deck crew were lost in concentration as they methodically took *Playboy* through the diving routine.

The young Radar Officer, assigned as wet nurse to the observers, strolled the length of the deck, smiling and giving pleasant nods calculated to put the tyro submariners at ease during the unique experience of being dropped below the ocean's surface. Boysie shifted in his seat. They seemed to have been busy doing nothing for an awfully long while—and they were not even allowed to smoke. Boysie found this kind of inactivity disturbing. There was nothing he could do; nothing he really understood about the submarine; no action he could take. He was even more disturbed by the fact that, at this last stage, he was still on his own. No trace of the opposition agent, or of the plan which was *Operation Understrike*, had come to him. He put back his head, closed his eyes and swallowed hard, trying to push down the apprehension which nagged at him like a poisoned foreign body throbbing and biting into his stomach wall. Uninvited, a childhood memory came flitting back—Christmas and being taken to see Santa Claus in Davy Jones' locker at a big store. The lift had been done up like a submarine and he was frightened by the paper octopi and squirming fish attached to the walls of the basement. They had taken him out and he had not even got his gift from Santa's waterproof sack. The present dilemma returned. In a few hours they would be preparing to fire the *Trepholite*. Something would happen soon. Boysie wished heartily that he was back, crying, in that big store basement.

The Radar Officer was now handing out waxed paper cups of coffee, obtained from a streamlined automatic dispenser near the rear bulkhead. The coffee burned through the paper cup and Boysie upset half—soaking the right knee of his slacks. The sound of orders, leisurely transmitted, came from the Control Deck.

"Operational depth."

"On, sir."

"Forward sonar operating."

"Clear ahead."

"Thank you. Check me clear on sonar every five minutes, please."

"Aye-aye, sir."

"Full ahead."

"Full ahead, sir. On. Maintaining full ahead."

"Course set and constant."

"Aye-aye, sir. Course set and constant."

Below Boysie, the seat quivered to the ostinato rhythm of the turbines. The big air-conditioning ducts along the starboard side—above the two curved doors marked in red "Escape Tubes One and Two"—whirred efficiently. It was all very professional, ultra precise, thorough, steady and deadly, thought Boysie. But something was going to happen. Soon it would come. Death? Destruction? Anti-climax? Soon.

THE CHIEF did not get into his office until after eleven on the Monday morning. He was in a filthy temper and bilious (the food had been good and rare in Hampshire). Consequently, the Chief did not do his usual scan of the DO's week-end reports until the late afternoon. Even then it was only by chance that his eye happened to catch the note about Mostyn and San Diego.

"Strewth!" exclaimed the Chief grabbing for the telephone.

There was an hour's delay for transatlantic calls—even on the closed line.

"Well, cut me in or something, you stupid whore," he bellowed at the operator—who happened to be a devout Roman Catholic with two brothers in the priesthood and an aunt who was next in line for Mother Superior of an enclosed order of nuns near Leatherhead. "This is Top-Top-over-the-bloody-Top Priority." The Chief, always concerned for his neck, was almost at panic stations.

IT WAS twelve noon; seventy fathoms down, approximately forty-five miles due West of San Diego. The big motors were stopped and *Playboy* was lined up in the firing position. The US Navy observer and Rondinelli, the Security man, were returning to the Observation Deck after completing their guided visit round Captain O'Hara's domain.

"Next two, please, sir," said the Radar Officer.

"You go first, Oakes, and I'll follow in the rear," said Braddock-Fairchild, smiling at the Army Major and 'Tiger', the Wing-Commander.

"Just as you like," said the Army Major.

"OK by me," said the Wing-Commander.

The Radar Officer wandered across to the American

137

observers and started chatting to Rondinelli about the boredom of life in the Submarine Service.

Braddock-Fairchild leaned back, his lips an inch from Boysie's left ear.

"You know what to do, don't you?" said Commander Braddock-Fairchild, RN.

The question came so casually that it took Boysie a moment to realise its implications. Then the shock caught hold of his system. He felt like a badly made Gelée Hachée. This was impossible. Ridiculous.

"I beg your pardon?" said Boysie shakily.

"I said, you know what to do, don't you?"

It was not impossible. The old salt was his opposition contact.

"No," answered Boysie, the reply coming out like a catarrhal cough—a knotted ball of tension building up, strangling guts, windpipe, the lot. He still had not really grasped it. Priscilla's Pa on the other side? No. But yes. And Boysie still had not the faintest idea what *Operation Understrike* entailed.

Braddock-Fairchild was alert, worry flecking his eyes.

"Didn't Gorilka brief you?"

"Yes . . . I mean no . . . You're with . . .?" Boysie groped for the correct words, re-thinking himself into the role of opposition agent. ". . . You're with us?"

"Of course. Didn't he even tell you that?"

"Said someone would contact me. What's it all about?" Boysie was speaking in his normal voice.

"Keep it down, you fool. Oh God. Bloody oaf, Gorilka," hissed Braddock-Fairchild. "Suppose it's all Khavichev's fault. Whenever he gets a new toy he has to play with it. No patience. That's why we're stuck with you. Well, quickly, listen to me. You're armed, I hope?"

Boysie nodded. He would have to see this through. Before putting the fix on Braddock-Fairchild, he would have to go along with him—as far as he was able. At least he had to find out the object of the operation. He did not even dare denounce the Commander. Lord knew who else was working for the opposition—in here or on the Control Deck. Braddock-Fairchild was whispering rapidly.

"You're here to assist with the take-over. O'Hara will collapse . . ." (Perhaps O'Hara was in it as well, thought Boysie) ". . . When he does, I'll deal with the radio and close the bulkhead. You get the Navigation Officer and anyone else you can. It'll probably be a free-for-all. We'll have to move fast. Just stand by me, and remember—ruthless!"

Boysie nodded unhappily. This was really playing it by ear. "You are an opposition agent . . . You are an opposition agent . . . You are an opposition agent . . . Think like one . . . Act like one . . . You are . . ." Boysie silently tried to motivate himself into his part.

EVERYTHING SEEMED relaxed and easy on the Control Deck when they stepped through the bulkhead.

"Good day, Commander. Good day, Mr Oakes. Happy to see you aboard." Captain O'Hara shepherded them towards the centre of the curved control desk.

"So this is where you press the button?" Braddock-Fairchild did not appear to be in the least bit nervous. Boysie could feel his own thighs shaking.

"Well, Commander, it's not so much a question of pressing buttons." They were standing directly behind the Ballistics Officer now. "Our first shot, as you know, will be on the aircraft. In the centre here you'll see the ICD Mk IV Homer setting control." In the middle of the Ballistics Officer's section of the desk, set apart from the other instruments by an inlaid circle of metal, was a small knob below a quarter-curved panel graded with numbers from one to five. The knob operated a sharp black and white needle. The needle pointed to the number four. "The setting is child's play," continued O'Hara, "In fact the ICD Mk IV could be operated by a five-year-old—as I am often telling Jimmy here." Jimmy, the Ballistics Officer, laughed like a man who has had the same joke made about him many times before. O'Hara went on.

"There are five corresponding series on which the Homer

can operate. One to five marked on this dial. The Homer in the target aircraft is—we hope—set to number four. So ours is also set to four. When we get notification that the aircraft is on course, Jimmy here switches on to the pre-selected count-down," the switch was marked in brilliant red above the ICD panel. "From there on the firing is automatic and nothing on this earth can stop it. When the Homer in *Trepholite's* nose picks up the corresponding Homer we get a winking light up here." His hand moved high above the desk. Boysie could distinguish the small red bulb among the regimented dials. "When that starts blinking you know that blast-off will occur within sixty seconds. And I'm not even going to try and explain how . . ."

"Please don't. There are times when I feel I would have been happier in Nelson's navy." Braddock-Fairchild smiled warmly: the look of one who eternally muddles through. "What about the guided shot?"

"Yea, well, I was just coming to that. It's more complicated, of course . . ."

"Before you start, do have a ju-jube, Captain. I know they're your weakness . . ." Braddock-Fairchild was holding a small plastic bag. There was a laugh from the Navigation Officer.

"Well, thank you, Commander." O'Hara reached forward. "They're my Navigation Officer's weakness as well."

"You have one too." Braddock-Fairchild offered the bag to the Navigation Officer. "Anyone else?"

"I don't mind. Thank you," from the Ballistics Officer. He took a third sweet and popped it into his mouth.

Boysie could do nothing to stop what happened next. Brad-dock-Fairchild dropped the bag and stepped back. Boysie reached for the Makarov in his slacks pocket. The move was in-stinctive. In a second something was going to blow. But he had no idea what he was going to do about it. A choking sound came from the Captain who had both hands up to his throat. The Navigation Officer was trying to get out of his seat, gulping for air. Now the Ballistics Officer. O'Hara bent double and fell. There was a shout from the far end of the control desk. The

Electronics Officer was moving. The Navigation and Ballistics Officers were both down now, writhing on the deck, next to their Captain: all three making noises like young pigs in an abattoir. Boysie heard a clang as Braddock-Fairchild closed the heavy bulkhead door; then a violent crash and the smell of cordite; then two more. Boysie had no chance to look round: the Electronics Officer and the Coxswain were diving at him. Out of self-defence, Boysie had his gun up. He tried to shout, but the Electronics Officer was nearly up to him. Boysie sidestepped; the man tripped and Boysie brought his pistol butt down hard. The Electronics Officer gave a winded "Hu!", and fell across the Ballistics Officer's legs. The Coxswain had passed Boysie, making for Braddock-Fairchild. There was another shot—sounding, in the confined space, like a bazooka shell. Boysie turned to see the Coxswain lurch forward grabbing at his stomach. He ended up in a heap by the Communications Officer's seat.

Boysie's first reflex was to pump every bullet in the Makarov's magazine at Braddock-Fairchild, who was leaning, panting, against the tightly-shut bulkhead. But common sense somehow held his trigger finger. The Control Deck looked like the final act of a bad Elizabethan drama. O'Hara, and the Navigation and Ballistics Officers lay dreadfully still. The radio equipment had been shattered by two bullets and the young Communications Officer was slumped forward on the desk. There was a lot of blood round his neck. The Coxswain was certainly dead, and the Electronics Officer was going to be out for a long while. Boysie stupidly hoped that he had not hit him too hard. He felt horribly cold. Shock would not yet let him think about the terrible part he had automatically played in this carnage. He willed himself to think about essentials. He had to find out what Braddock-Fairchild had been instructed to do. The Commander was over on the starboard side now, fiddling with something high above the escape tubes, which were positioned as on the Observation Deck.

"Well done, Solev," he was saying. "We were lucky, I didn't expect three of 'em to take the cyanide sweeties." He seemed to have found what he was looking for. "This is the one, I think. Yes." Boysie came up close behind him. The Commander was removing a small inspection hatch cover—quickly unscrewing the four small butterfly nuts that kept it in place.

"Air conditioning," said Braddock-Fairchild. He had the hatch cover off.

"Hold it, will you; and give it back quickly when I shout."

Boysie, still stunned by the sudden slaughter that surrounded them, obediently took the small oblong of metal.

"Quickly! Close the vents."

Boysie looked around. Fuddled.

"Oh, all right you fool. Do it meself." Braddock-Fairchild stretched up to an hexagonal knob above the air conditioning vents and turned it in a series of sharp jerking movements. The ventilator flanges began to close. None of the air piped throughout the ship would be pumped into the Control Room.

"Don't want the stuff bowling us over in here. Plenty of air to last until we leave."

The Commander's hand dipped into a pocket, bringing out a tubular plastic container about an inch long and quarter of an inch in diameter. Unscrewing the cap, he tipped two round glass phials into the palm of his right hand. Dropping the container to the floor, the Commander pushed his hand through the air conditioning hatch. Boysie heard a crunch as the phials broke on the inside of the pipe.

"Quick. The cover." The Commander replaced it—screwing the nuts tightly in place. "Right, that'll fix anyone else living and breathing on board. Right through the whole system. Be sprayed out of all the vents."

"What . . . What was it?"

"Not quite sure. Mild nerve gas of some kind. Gorilka provided it. Now, we've got a lot to do, Solev. A lot." He was over at the Captain's position on the control desk. Searching. "Here we are. HK 5 off." The hand slammed down on the two Beam-Bender switches. "HK 5 on. Good. Now they won't get an accurate fix on us."

Boysie could stand no more of this. The shock was wearing

off. If Gorilka had provided it, the odds were that the gas now being pumped through *Playboy's* air conditioning ducts was lethal. He had stood by—no, assisted—while five men had died in here. Now he had helped to kill his colleagues behind the bulkhead door—and lord knew how many crew. Everything had happened so fast. If only he had thought about it: anticipated. He should have realised that Braddock-Fairchild was the only opposition agent on board. And he had let this happen. Just stood there incapable. Incompetent. Impotent.

"Oh Christ!" moaned Boysie internally.

He lifted the Makarov pistol and pointed it unsteadily at the Commander's back.

"Just turn round from there and get your hands up," he said, surprised that his voice sounded so calm.

Braddock-Fairchild stiffened. He did not turn or attempt to move, but just stood there, his big brown hands resting on the control desk.

"So," said the Commander. "You're defecting again are you, Solev. Gorilka told me to be careful with you. He warned me."

"I'm not Solev. Gorilka's boys got the wrong man. My name really *is* Oakes." He felt as though a column of red ants were marching up his spine—shod in snow-drenched boots. He heard the Commander's intake of breath. Over-confident, Boysie lowered his gun and started to move forward. There was a flurry of movement and a violent roar. Boysie felt himself being spun round against the hull. The Makarov was whisked out of his hand and he was going dizzy, clutching at his arm. Braddock-Fairchild had been quick, the automatic was still dribbling smoke. Boysie, down on one knee, could feel the blood trickling out of the wound high in his right arm. The old boy had been reasonably accurate.

"I should really finish you off now," said the Commander. Strange, thought Boysie, through the pain and haze, his voice still had that very English upper-crust quarter deck growl. You did not associate that kind of voice with Commie sympathisers.

"But I think it might be better for you to go with the rest of them," continued Braddock-Fairchild. "When *Playboy*

143

explodes. It will be far more terrifying for you. And probably much more painful. Just desserts. Oakes, Just desserts."

Boysie's vision was going—grey, then the black nothing of unconsciousness.

THEY GOT Birdlip out of the Main Control Centre, to take the transatlantic call, at about the same time as the police car —siren wailing—came bucketing up to the Main Gate of North Island Base. In the back of the car, white, haggard and tired, next to Police Captain Boyle, sat Chicory Triplehouse.

VII–... STRIKE

BIRDLIP was a man in anguish. In the very centre of his conscience he knew that he had done the right thing. All available information had led him to mistrust the Englishman, Mostyn. Birdlip morbidly reflected that he had practised the techniques of mental cruelty on Mostyn. He had brow-beaten him with words; sneered at him; been sarcastic; bullied and cajoled him. Then, in a matter of minutes, the world of Rupert Birdlip crumpled. A telephone call from England told him that this was *the* Mostyn—2IC of Special Security. To add to his woe, a peachy dame corroborated Mostyn's story about the body in Room 30 at the Sleepy Bear motel. Birdlip just did not know where to look. He was, in fact, looking at the top of his desk. Mostyn, still exuding an air of deep injury, sat to his left. Across the room was lovely Miss Chicory Triplehouse. ("An amateur," Mostyn had said, "employed by our New York man as an occasional courier. Didn't really know what she was letting herself in for.") She had told her story—from the moment that she was assigned as Boysie's escort, until the previous night, when the police had picked her up uncommonly plastered in the bar at San Diego airport.

Chicory had, of course, disobeyed Boysie and gone to look at the cadaver. The experience had closed the circuit, causing mild shock; and on reaching the airport, Chicory had done nothing about getting herself a seat on a New York flight. Instead, she had gone to the bar and consumed highball after potent highball. First she had become maudlin, cried a little, and called the bartender "Joe". But when—rather late on the Sunday night—she had started to remove her stockings, as a prelude to even more revealing divestiture, the barman had called the cops.

Chicory had awakened, late and uncomfortable, in the drunk tank at the City Jail. In the cold light of a hot hangover, she yelled for a policeman and babbled about a dead man in Room 30. Chicory's statement was startling—particularly as the entire San Diego police force had spent a good deal of time laughing over the nut who had sent their Captain trailing after a non-existent body. Now, telling her story to Mostyn and Birdlip, she thought of something else.

"So it must have been Boysie, not Vladimir, who came on down here," she said. "Boysie was the only one who knew about Max in New York. Vladimir had never heard of him. Yet I distinctly remember him saying 'Call Max when you get back to New York.' It must have been Vladimir who was killed in the bed." She was still near the hysterical fringe—the voice un-controlled in the higher register.

Then something else struck her. She had not bothered to mention her sexual adventures—not in any detail that is. But Mostyn, having that sort of mind, had worked out a fairly ac-curate picture for himself.

"That bastard, Boysie," thought Chicory. "He must've changed places. Geez, no wonder I thought they were so much alike. The rat!"

Mostyn said, "You all right, Miss Triplehouse? You look a bit flushed."

Mostyn hoped that she was right about Boysie, for, though he caused the 2IC more agony than any other member of the Department, Boysie was his particular creation. Out of a lump of provincial clay, Mostyn had moulded this man; breathed the breath of life into him; dressed him in fine raiment, and set him to work. Any psychiatrist would have also told Mostyn that he did not want to lose Boysie because it was through Boysie he could release the most sadistic and power-ridden facets of his personality.

Birdlip, who had been very quiet until now, broke into the conversation. "Colonel Mostyn, don't you think that we should really do something about *Playboy*? No matter if it's the Commie or your man on board."

146

"There is only one thing to do—as I have been repeatedly telling you, old Birdmouth . . ."

". . . Lip."

". . . Lip. *Playboy* will have to be recalled. Game postponed owing to heavy machinations and an *agent provocateur* on the pitch. Should have thought you'd have already done something about that. Time like an ever-rolling stream and all that jazz."

Birdlip braced himself. "I think, Colonel, it would come better from you."

"What would?"

"The news . . . That the trials should be cancelled. Admiral Fullenhaft ain't going to be too . . ."

"Pleased. No. I'll bet: and you don't want to be at the receiving end of his just wrath, old Bird . . ."

"lip . . ."

"Yes."

Chicory was left in the Guard Room, happy with three very tall and manly Marines, while Mostyn and Birdlip jeeped it up to the Main Control Centre, from which the *Playboy-Trepholite* trials were being directed.

During the past twenty-four hours, Mostyn had been given a lot of time to think. He had approached the problem from every angle, and still intuitively felt that there was something of sinister importance about the whole affair. He could not settle for plain healthy sabotage, or the theft of *Playboy*. Just behind his conscious thoughts lurked the Coelacanth, the missing link, which would not come to the surface.

The Control Centre was a long airy room with a wide glass wall reaching high to the ceiling and looking out to sea. About a hundred men and women, engaged in a complicated multitude of duties—from watching radar scanners to checking computers—were working with concentrated efficiency. At a central dais, above a vast chart of the Californian coast and the immediate Pacific, sat Admiral Charles Fullenhaft. Initially the Admiral was pleased to see Birdlip and Mostyn. This stage of the operation was routine and boring. Admiral Fullenhaft was a great one for 'company'. But as Mostyn talked, so the Admiral became uneasy. From uneasiness his face became grave. Before Mostyn could finish his appreciation of the situation, the Admiral took action and picked up his hand microphone. The voice came deadly over the Control Centre loudspeaker system.

"Admiral Fullenhaft speaking. Commander Stenway, will you recall *Playboy:* action immediate. This operation is postponed. And look, George, don't have any truck with that sonofabitch O'Hara. Just get him back here. Tell him to surface and come home pronto. All sections relay that."

Commander Stenway, in charge of Communications—way down the room to their left—looked startled and then began talking fast to his underlings. Fullenhaft turned to Mostyn.

"That satisfy you, Colonel?"

"I think it's the only thing to do, sir. I won't be satisfied until *Playboy's* back and my boy's face to face with me."

"My, God, it'd better be the only thing to do. I'll be the laughing stock of the United States Navy—not to mention the Submarine Service—if it isn't."

Mostyn was watching the Communications Section across the room. There seemed to be a good deal of activity going on. Far more than was warranted by a simple recall order. He saw Commander Stenway pick up his microphone.

"Stenway, sir. We cannot raise *Playboy*. They seem to have gone off the air."

The Admiral gave Mostyn a quick glance of alarm.

"When did you last have them?"

"Fifteen minutes ago. The normal quarter-hourly check."

"OK. Radar?"

The officer in charge of radar had already been in puzzled conference with his staff.

"We're getting a mighty odd reaction here, Admiral. Looks as if Captain O'Hara's got the HK5 operating."

"What's the HK5?" Mostyn whispered to Birdlip.

"Radar Beam-Bender."

Another voice came over the speaker system.

"Both the Grumman Trackers report heavy radar interference consistent to HK5 device, Admiral."

"Hell!" said Fullenhaft, looking at Mostyn. "What d'we do now, sonny?" It was a long time since Mostyn had been addressed as 'sonny'. He didn't much care for it.

"It looks as though we're too late, sir."

"Yes." The Admiral was on the brink of big decisions. "What subs have we on standby?" he asked his ADC.

The ADC, true to that breed, had things at his fingertips. "*Scabardfish* and *Seacat*, sir."

"Make me a signal. Admiral Fullenhaft to Director Naval Operations Pacific Fleet. Request *Scabardfish* and *Seacat*, under way immediate. Surface, course due West at speed and await orders."

"Shall we move in some of the PT-Boats, sir? They're nearest," said the ADC.

Mostyn followed the Admiral's eyes down to the chart. *Playboy's* position was marked by a blue plastic submarine which looked as though it had come out of a cereal packet. Other ships and aircraft were similarly marked. Mostyn could see that eight of the fast little PT-Boats were deployed in a circle of about three miles radius around *Playboy*.

"No," said the Admiral. "For God's sake keep the firing area clear. Put a stop to that target aircraft and notify the helicopters to maintain their position. We don't want the choppers moving over the area. If they do happen to loose off a *Trepholite* and there's a 'copter on top, the meeting ain't going to be a happy one."

There it was. The click in Mostyn's head at the words 'top' and 'meeting'. *Topmeet*. The Prime Minister. "Ye Gods!" said Mostyn looking at the date inset on his watch. That figured. It was just possible. In his mind, Mostyn was doing some simple arithmetic involving flight times, speeds and altitudes.

The Admiral was speaking to him.

"We've got a flight of missile interceptors, 'bout a 100 miles North West of *Playboy's* firing position. I'm going to move them in just in case we get a *Trepholite* going astray. Though I

149

doubt if they will be able to stop one. That missile's pretty fool-proof."

"It's not armed though, is it?" asked Mostyn, as coolly as the tension would allow.

"No, but if one happened to go astray inland it could plough up a mighty big patch of real estate."

"And if it hit an aircraft?"

"Write off. Impact would blow an airplane right out of the sky. Why?"

"Oh nothing." Casual: Mostyn did not want to start a panic. For one thing he did not know who was supposed to be appraised about *Topmeet*. "Admiral, d'you think I could possibly have a scrambled line to your security boys in San Francisco?" Mostyn hoped that he did not sound too worried.

THERE WAS a snake around his arm. A mammoth Mamba coiled from his wrist. It was biting high up near the shoulder. Boysie lashed out with his left hand. The pain was like a white-hot twisting branding-iron. Boysie moaned and opened his eyes. Then he remembered. The pain was real enough. The top of his arm throbbed with great regular punches—juddering stabs to a steady beat. The back of his throat felt dry, and a Black and Decker power drill seemed to be easing its way through his frontal lobes. Boysie screwed up his eyes—as though trying to swill the pain from behind them. Slowly he raised his lids again, lifting his head. He was propped against the bulkhead. A more definite focus returned. He could see a pair of shoes—too heavy, with large rounded toes. A square, thought Boysie. His eyes moved upwards. Commander Braddock-Fairchild, RN, was sitting in the Captain's chair, swivelled round to face him, the automatic pistol lying on his lap. The old pirate was smiling.

"Glad you've wakened up, Oakes. In time for the fun, eh?" said the Commander, the smile changing to a leer.

Boysie tried to muster energy, then realised that he did not care very much. Someone had once told him that dying from severe injuries, or a serious disease, was easy. You were too weak and tired to care. He looked at his arm. This is stupid, he thought, beginning to live a little. It's only a flesh wound; you're not going to die from that. Then he remembered the Commander's last words before unconsciousness: "It might be better for you to go with the rest of them when *Playboy* explodes." As memory returned so did fear; and with it Boysie realised a terrible hatred for Braddock-Fairchild.

"I suppose your precious Priscilla's in on this?" was all he could think of.

The Commander stopped smiling—a squall among the heavy lines above his eyebrows. "No. Afraid Priscilla's never taken to her father. Knows very little about me really. Mother's girl. I never got on. Never got on with her mother come to think of it. But then nobody did."

"You're a bloody fine advertisement for Dartmouth aren't you?" Boysie seemed to be deliberately needling him. The Commander stared—eyes fixed and chilly. The look had a cutting edge.

"D'ye know, believe I am. The Country. The Service. Never been the same since the war. No guts. No drivin' power. No discipline. To me it's as though the whole British nation's been wallowing in a hot bath. All velvet, mixed up with leather, nylon underwear and cheap plastics. Vitality sapped. Affluence run riot. Everyone's an expert. No one's expert. All teach yourself, the free libraries, night school and the short course. England's an adaptation from an original country. All genuine imitation. No discipline." The voice was hard with belief. This was the political dogma of Communism translated into shining faith and misapplied. The Commander hated his own country and her political leanings like a saint loathes the very idea of sin. "No discipline." He repeated. "Only one country got it. Only one country to admire these days. Wonderful how they've pressed on. Had to of course. Still pioneers." He shook his head firmly. "England? Finished. Good God, man, you must see that. No goal. Not any more. Nothing to pioneer. Finished. Done for. New kind of colonialism now. Got to be ruthless to save mankind from itself."

"So you've left the sinking ship."

"Sensible thing to do. Never believed in going down with something that has become worthless. Got to progress. Got to search for a true and decent way of life."

Boysie tried to move himself into a more comfortable position. The Commander's hand dropped to the gun butt.

"It's all right. Just shifting."

Braddock-Fairchild looked at his watch. "Haven't got long to wait anyway. Ten minutes. Fifteen at the most. But of course you don't really know what it's all about do you?"

"Nobody's had the courtesy to tell me."

"Shame. I put your mind at rest? Be in the best fictional tradition eh? Minutes slipping away while villain explodes evil plot." Braddock-Fairchild was smiling again. Then the man's features went suddenly grave, as though someone had pulled a switch. "Well! The Prime Minister's getting the chop to begin with."

Silence. To Boysie it seemed a remote thought. Remote and absurd.

"What d'ye think about that?"

"There'd be some who'd say you were doing the country a service."

The Commander nodded agreement. "Yes. Quite. That's why he's only an incidental factor." A smile like a rasher cut on number five of the slicer. "Did you listen to any of Admiral Fullenhaft's briefing, or were you asleep all the time?" He did not expect an answer. "Much of what he said was accurate. Too accurate. Didn't mention, of course, that they've got the hulls laid down for seven *Playboy Class* submarines. Didn't mention that *Trepholite* is ready to go into full production. D'ye remember he said the *Playboy-Trepholite* complex gave the Americans the edge on any navy in the world? Well, that's the truth. The literal, exact truth. And in this game of the nuclear balance of power it is a factor of vital importance. Y'see?" Boysie shifted again. The hard old hand tightened round the automatic. The voice never faltered. "Real advance is this miniature warhead. *Dies Irae*. Remarkable. Size of warheads always been a problem. All the major countries been working on them. All want high-powered rockets with warheads no bigger than a walnut producing Hiroshima plus 1000 bang. Well, Americans have gone ahead in that race." An almost furtive grin moved across the weathered face. "But it seemed a pity—when I was right on the spot—to let them *keep* ahead. Original plan was to disrupt the trials and dispose of a lot of people concerned with the *Playboy-Trepholite* project. Redirect *Playboy's Trepholites*, on a low-angle trajectory, at a couple of targets on North Island. Then blow *Playboy*. Without warheads could still've knocked out lots of the top men. Two of the things—with boosters going—crashing into the Control Room back at the Base. Make a rousing accident. Nasty mess."

"Yes," said Boysie without enthusiasm. He could imagine the small-scale havoc two runaway missiles would cause.

"But that was before the Prime Minister and his travelling companion. 'Bout a fortnight ago. Changed all plans. Moscow went mad. Then you turned up as well. That was a mistake. Complicated the issue."

"Oh?" Boysie's arm seemed to have become less painful. Or his senses were getting used to the throbbing.

"You keep abreast of politics, Oakes? Or is the political scene something you choose to ignore—like most of the British ostriches?"

Boysie kept his mouth closed. Braddock-Fairchild hardly stopped for breath.

"If you read the newspapers—which I doubt by the look of you—you will know that your Minister of Defence is at present having talks with the President of the United States of America. You'll also know that the PM's recently taken it into his head to make unscheduled visits to consult with the President. Some say he can't make a decision by himself."

Boysie nodded. "Others say he's trying to keep his left hand from knowing what his right hand is doing."

"Twelve weeks ago. Three-day conference in Washington. Nothing announced until the PM was safely back in Downing Street."

Boysie knew all about that one. VIPSEC* had been going wild about the Prime Minister's cloak and dagger operations. Mostyn had been called in to do a lot of oil pouring.

"Couple of weeks ago," the Commander went on, "he arranged another of these clandestine meetings. A big one. Only a handful of people in the know—security, airline, and, of course, the organisation which employs me. We planted a man close to the present Head of State years ago. When he was only one of the bright, rising boys. Just on the off chance. Years ago. Long before I saw the light. Fellow's paid dividends."

"Proper little Co-op," muttered Boysie.

"And this time. For this visit—our man with the PM tells us—he's bringing a little friend with him. Bunch of the North Island boffins flying off to meet them after the trials."

"Well?"

"Ever heard of Dr Lund?"

"Adolph Lund?" Complete uncontrolled anxiety.

"Adolph Lund," repeated the Commander.

Boysie certainly had heard of Dr Adolph Lund. It was Mostyn himself who had supervised the German nuclear physicist's spiriting from East to West Berlin. The protection of Adolph Lund had been on the Top Priority list ever since. Boysie had even done a short stint with the security staff who kept the doctor in his scientific cocoon—surrounded by barbed wire and guard dogs—deep in the heart of Essex. Boysie had been forced to leave that particular duty after only two days, following an unfortunate incident with one of the guard dogs with whom he had inadvertently tangled. Animals always seemed to spot the timid side of Boysie. But Lund, a scientific recluse, was said to be Britain's most valuable spoil from behind the Curtain. Single handed he had resolved the early teething troubles of the Frobisher Tracker Rocket. And Boysie thought he remembered hearing something about a project for scaling down nuclear warheads. Braddock-Fairchild was talking again.

"Lund, you know, is the real reason why America has gone

* VIPSEC: VIP Security, a small sub-section of the Department of Special Security which deals with the co-ordination of other departments regarding security measures for British VIPs.

154

ahead in the race for the effective small warhead. Lund was working on it behind the Curtain before he decided to play traitor and run to the West. Put my friends months behind, while America got the answer—in spite of the fact that your people kept Lund in purdah. But we'll catch up with America. Soon we'll catch up. Lund left a lot of papers behind. Only a matter of time. Matter of months." He paused to swallow noisily. "Not the point now. Dr Lund, we hear has already dated *Trepholite*. Claims to have the basic design for a warhead only half the size, and twice as powerful, as *Dies Irae*. See what that means? Puts the West two jumps ahead instead of one. Can't have that. Oh no." He began to speak very slowly and distinctly. "And Adolph Lund, who never moves, who is never seen, who is guarded more closely than the Crown Jewels, is coming out of his shell—travelling with the Prime Minister to meet the President. Obvious why. England again. Has the most astute scientific brain in the field and can't afford to develop any of the brain's products . . ."

"And what the hell's this got to with *Playboy*? Here and now what's it got to do with it?" Boysie cut in.

"Ah!" Braddock-Fairchild looked happy. "Just so happens that today's the day. Prime Minister's flying with Lund to meet the President now. This very moment. Boeing 707 chartered from BOAC. Not direct London-New York or London-Washington either. Coming over the Pole to San Francisco. President and Minister of Defence flew down quietly last night. Big get-together. Large nuclear brain conference due in San José this afternoon. Point is, that the PM's aircraft passes only 400 miles north of us. Very soon. Few minutes. Irreparable loss to the West. Great statesman and very great scientist. Priceless brace to bag in one afternoon, what?"

A gut-somersault for Boysie. "And you're going to . . .?"

"Yes. *Trepholite* fitted with ICD Homer will home on the aircraft." The Commander seemed almost complacent.

"But how . . .?"

"Have friends. Told you we have a man very close. Homer's quite small you know. Planted nicely in the baggage before

155

take-off. Set to number five. If you were able to come over here you'd see I've set our Homer to number five. Switched on pre-selected count-down. Nothing'll stop it now. Prime Minister's aeroplane'll be in range any minute. Little red light'll start blinking. Then whoosh! Won't stand a chance."

Boysie was doing some mental overtime, urging brain and body into action. But he seemed to be helpless. The repercussions of this could be enormous. Lund's death might well, within a month or so, drastically affect the delicate balance of power. He would certainly be a disastrous loss. Apart from that, there was the aspect of the Prime Minister's mode of death. Flying to a secret meeting with the President of the United States and killed by a stray missile fired from an American submarine. Public feeling would run high. The whole business could cause a serious rift in the Anglo-American alliance, and a drag on the nuclear advance.

"But what about you? How . . .?"

"Easy enough. *Playboy* has a scuttling mechanism. Blow the thing to tiny pieces. Call it the *Omega Switch*. Very fond of names like that—the Americans. *Omega Switch*. Had to rifle O'Hara's body for the key, but it's in there." He pointed to a small drawer which had been pulled out from the under-side of the desk, between the Captain's position and that which should have been occupied by the Ballistics Officer.

"Time-fuse and switch in there. When *Trepholite* leaves us I set time-fuse to *Omega* minus thirty minutes. Press down on the switch. Put on my P50 mask. Into the escape tube and away."

"They'll catch up with you. You can't possibly . . ."

"Most of the contingencies've been taken care of. Originally had some problems because Lund and the PM weren't going to fly until four hours later. Couldn't afford to hang around in this state. At the mercy of the weather as well. Still. Gone very smoothly really. Not all clockwork. You for instance. Told Gorilka I didn't like the arrangements with Solev. Khavichev's idea, of course; felt he had to use Solev once they found you were coming down here. Idea was that Solev could take over if

I got knocked out. Suppose Gorilka expected me to brief you. Khavichev's slipping though, goes at things like a bull at a gate. That's what they say about Khavichev—between you and me—has a tendency to waste men. Still, suppose if you were going to be in *Playboy* anyway, when the balloon went up, he would never have had any opportunity to use Solev. Pity Gorilka bungled that one." He looked at his watch again. Getting nervous? Boysie wondered.

Then, without warning, high up on the instrument panel, the little red light began to blink rapidly. The corresponding Homers had made contact. In sixty seconds or less, *Trepholite* would be streaking towards the Boeing 707 in which the Prime Minister of Great Britain was, at that moment, engrossed in reading a spy thriller—about an amateur secret agent: a solicitor with a passion for antique traction engines. Behind him, a small, grey-faced little man was half-way through Kierkegaard's *Enten-Eller*. He seemed to be enjoying it.

BRADDOCK-FAIRCHILD was off guard. As the red light began to wink its warning, so his head automatically turned towards the control panel. This was Boysie's last chance. He jerked his knees upwards, and coiled his body for the spring. A wide sheet of pain sliced into his shoulder. Then, Braddock-Fairchild was whirling round on the swivel chair, the automatic pistol, an extension of his hand, prodding forward. Confused, Boysie saw that the Commander was not turning towards him, but swinging to his right.

There were two shots—great bursting thunderclaps echoing up the metal walls—followed by the whang of a ricochet. Then another shot. On his feet now, propelled forward by the initial effort of his leap. Boysie saw Braddock-Fairchild's eyes widen in that momentous change from life to death. The pistol slipped from him and fell with a scraping clatter, bouncing against the legs of the dead Ballistics Officer. Then, the Commander pitched forward over the tangle of bodies that lay between Boysie and the control desk.

Boysie stumbled over the communal pile of arms and legs,

still making for the desk. From behind, to his right, came a long shivering moan of pain. He reached the control desk, and glanced round. The Electronics Officer, whom Boysie had so violently slugged in the mêlée after O'Hara's collapse, was propped on one arm, Boysie's Makarov pistol—Braddock-Fairchild's last enemy—in his free hand.

The red light was still winking. It seemed to be going faster —as though heading for terminal action. Boysie hesitated before doing the only thing that made sense to his perplexed mind. His good arm reached out to the Homer Setting Dial. He twisted. The needle moved slowly off the number five setting. Boysie wrenched hard. The needle flicked right across the graded dial to number one. The red light went out. With any luck, Boysie thought, he had disconnected the Homer. He turned, leaning back against the desk—the pain slinking up and down his arm: heart tripping and breath wild.

With a mighty shake, the deck below him suddenly began to move. There was a deep rumble and, for a second, Boysie thought he was dropping once more into unconsciousness. The deck tilted to a low angle and everything seemed to be juddering! The noise—coming from somewhere for'ard—was like an underground train coming full belt into Oxford Circus. The deck was dropping under his feet now. Then, just as suddenly, there was stability and silence. Through the mist of pain, Boysie's mind closed round the facts. Disconnecting the Homer could not have arrested the firing sequence. The *Trepholite* had completed its blast-off.

Boysie lurched across to the Electronics Officer. Obviously, the man had come to; heard enough of the conversation to appreciate the dangerous situation, seen the Makarov—which had landed only a foot from his hand when Braddock-Fairchild's bullet caught Boysie's arm—and made the splendid effort which finished the Commander. When Boysie reached him, the Electronics Officer was almost unconscious again. He had been hit in the middle of the chest, and his breathing was now lapsing into that panting rattle which is the prelude to death.

MOSTYN FEROCIOUSLY rattled the telephone with the index finger of his right hand. They had put him in the small, sound-proof booth which housed the only scrambler phone in the Control Centre. Now he waited impatiently for Birdlip to clear him with United States Security in San Francisco. The seconds clicked past, about a hundred times less than their normal speed. The possible urgency seemed to slow time to a long drag of tension.

The phone clicked and a voice came on.

"Hallo. Colonel Mostyn?"

"Yes. Mostyn."

"Commander Birdlip's spoken to me, sir—Duty Officer. Who was it you wanted?"

"Anyone connected with *Topmeet*. Urgent!"

"Topmeet?" The American obviously did not recognise the codeword. "One moment, Colonel."

The second half of the twentieth century seemed to slip by. Then:

"Colonel Mostyn. You want either Jeffries or Ruddock. They're both out at the airfield."

"Well, get one of them for me. This is priority. Red emergency, for crying out loud."

"Yes sir; yes, Colonel."

The line went dead. Mostyn realised, with added alarm, that he was in desperate need of what his American colleagues artlessly called "The Little Boys' Room."

"RUDDOCK," SAID the voice, staccato, on the end of the line.

"Mostyn. British Special Security."

"Yea. They told me."

"Are you on *Topmeet*?"

"Yea. We're waitin' for the Man now."

"OK. Listen. Get that aircraft turned back . . . off-course . . . anything . . . but move it . . . There's a possible attempt to . . ." Mostyn stopped. Outside the booth, Birdlip was waving his arms. The Control Centre seemed to have gone crazy. Birdlip wrenched the door open.

"Colonel. They've fired one. They've launched a *Trepholite*."

"Oh my God!" Something else struck Mostyn. "Can't they destroy from here . . . Blow the thing up in the air?"

"No. Destroy button's in *Playboy*. Admiral's got the jets after it but we don't know what course the thing's tracking yet."

Ruddock's voice was coming, thin and plaintive, from the telephone.

"Hallo . . . Colonel Mostyn . . . Hallo . . . What's going on . . .?"

Mostyn brought the instrument up to his ear. "Try and turn the PM's aircraft off-course," he said quietly. "But I think it's too late."

Mostyn put down the telephone and followed Birdlip into the Control Centre.

"She's gone straight up, but doesn't seem to have set any operational course," said the Admiral when they reached the dais. Into his microphone, "You boys in radar got anything yet?"

A voice over the loudspeaker, "Green Flight moving into area at 36,000 feet."

Then, urgently, another voice, "Admiral, she's out of control. Winging down West and falling. *Trepholite's* uncontrolled. Looks like a spiral."

"Mark point of impact," said Admiral Charles Fullenhaft, cool and relieved.

THE TREPHOLITE came sizzling out of the sky to land exactly 315.8 miles south-west of San Diego in a patch of, happily, uninhabited sea.

AT 13.38 hours the Boeing 707 landed at San Francisco airport. A large closed car drove out to meet the jet as it taxied in. The Prime Minister of Great Britain, oblivious to his brush with mortality, hurried down the steps and into the car. Behind him came the little grey man—Adolph Lund.

In San José, the President of the United States was informed, by telephone, that his guests had arrived safely.

The Electronics Officer died soon after Boysie reached him. Prising the Makarov out of the vice-grip of the stiffening hand, Boysie pulled himself back to the Captain's swivel chair, where he sat surveying the grisly deckscape. He was walled up with death. In the past few days, he reflected, three others had died in his place—at least three others: Siedler, Solev, and now this young United States Navy officer who had shot Braddock-Fairchild at the crucial moment. Boysie was trembling, the pain enveloping his whole arm which hung like a spare part from his blood-soaked shoulder. Why the hell should he have been saved? Unless it was to die some more hideous death. It came to him that he was, in all truth, entombed in a watery grave. A couple of hundred feet below the surface in a metal hull stacked with corpses. He did not dare open the big bulkhead door leading to the Observation Deck—the invisible killer gas still probably lurked there. His left hand strayed to his chest. Of course! The P50 which had been slung, like a gas mask in its canvas bag, ever since they had boarded the submarine that morning. If Boysie wanted "out" he would have to play at being a human torpedo and go the way Braddock-Fairchild had intended—through the escape tube. There were plenty of small craft up there on the ceiling of the sea. He was bound to be picked up.

Less pleasant thoughts now began streaming into Boysie's consciousness—sharks, octopi, sting rays, mantas: the squirming fishy horrors of the deep. For a gruesomely imaginative moment, Boysie saw himself being ripped to pieces by the razor teeth of a pair of barracuda. Wholly chicken by this time, Boysie decided that it might be better to wait a while. Surely they would be starting some kind of rescue operation? Perhaps just one member of the crew had escaped the gas and decided to make the ascent. Boysie looked at his watch. It was barely one o'clock—less than an hour since Braddock-Fairchild had started the slaughter. He could afford to wait just ten, maybe twenty minutes. Half an hour even, he could wait.

Boysie remembered the HK5. Turning the chair, he searched for the switches, found them, and disconnected the beam-bending device. His mind was made up. He would wait. But, as the minutes ticked by, the reek of death started to play tricks. Twice he could have sworn Braddock-Fairchild's body moved. In the silence, he thought he heard breathing. Now, was the Communications Officer trying to raise his bloody head? This was *Macbeth* and a touch of the Capulets' Monument rolled into one. His heart was trying to find a gap in his ribs—the timpani at the opening of the *Brahms' First*. The pain was subdued again, but in its place had come a crawling under the skin: that big spider tickle up the short hairs at the nape of his neck.

After ten minutes he could stand the charnel house no longer. Unzipping the canvas bag on his chest, Boysie took out the P50 mask, and with knees of tacky jelly, lumbered towards the escape tubes, his brain tussling through the cobweb of events, trying to call back the drill taught him so meticulously by the submariners and the Marine sergeant only yesterday afternoon. As a lift for his depression and fear, Boysie played, ena-mena-mina-mo to choose which tube he should use. Number One was the winner.

A light came on near his feet as he closed the tube door—turning the small wheel until the bolt clicked audibly into place. Incongruously, Boysie thought of the little man whom, some said, lived in refrigerators to operate the light when you closed the door. The walls of the tube were snug and smooth against his shoulders, and he could not help thinking of the Human Cannonball he had once seen at Lord John Sangers Circus, years ago.

"One," he said to himself, "Inflate life jacket."

He pulled on the metal ring, and with a hiss acquired an extra few inches round the back and chest. He was now wedged tightly against the walls of the tube.

"Two. Put on P50." The mask fitted over his mouth, nose

and eyes—the eye-pieces separate so there was no misting up from breath, as with the old service gas-masks during the war. Fitting the mask took some time. Boysie found it difficult to get the thing comfortable using only one hand.

"Three. Equalise pressure." Which one was it for the pressure? The green lever or the red? Red. Boysie reached over with his left hand and threw the red switch. The pressure dial was fitted to the floor between his feet, like a bathroom weighing machine. The two needles, opposing one another, trembled and then crept round until they were in juxtaposition. This was it. Boysie took hold of his right wrist and tucked it into the waistband of his slacks, so that the damaged arm would be held close to his body. He took a deep breath, looked at the pressure once more, and firmly pulled down the green lever.

Nothing happened. Then, with a surging in his ears, Boysie felt his body being crushed; high walls of water squeezing him into a tiny ball. His knees came up and his back arched forward. Now the reverse—he was jack-knifed into a rigid position of attention. He seemed to be spinning . . . upwards and upwards . . . gulping for air . . . the popping sea-shell roar in his ears. Through the eye-piece there was nothing but blackness . . . upwards and upwards. Gulping for air . . . the roar . . . a heart-leap as he felt something bump his body. A shark? A dreaded barracuda? Lungs were hot . . . another gulp inside the mask. Still the spiral. It seemed to be going on for ever. How long since he pulled the lever? A minute? Five? Ten? Twenty? No. Seconds. Only seconds. He was wet . . . water crushing . . . then light . . . it was getting lighter at the end of the waterlogged elevator shaft. The singing roar began to lose volume. And with a frightening jerk, Boysie's head broke the surface and he was bobbing up and down with a warm breeze knocking gently against his cheek.

With his free arm, Boysie tore off the P50 mask. Everything was blue and swaying—the sky and the sea rolled into one, turning in a slow circle around him. Somewhere there was the sound of a motor—a steady buzz. The water was slopping into his mouth. He was going under again. Opening his eyes Boysie saw—what seemed to be a long way off—the dot of a small boat growing larger and larger. His head fell back, and Boysie Oakes again lost consciousness, his body buoyed up by the big yellow life-jacket.

Two little yellow plastic submarines had been moved across the operations' board and now lay in squares adjacent to the blue plastic submarine that was *Playboy*.

"*Scabardfish* and *Seacat* deployed five miles from firing area, sir."

"OK." The Admiral was looking at the chart. "Send *Seacat* in submerged. Put a diver out to examine *Playboy*. And tell him to keep clear of the launching tubes unless he wants to take a short course in astronomy."

"Aye-aye, sir."

The tension in the Control Centre had passed its peak. Mostyn just hoped nobody was going to loose off the other *Trepholite*. He kept thinking of Boysie—if it was Boysie. For all he knew, Boysie was responsible for firing the bloody thing.

"HK5 is off, sir. We've got *Playboy* clear on the scanner. Right in position—bull's eye for the firing area."

"I give up," said the Admiral. "What the hell's going on down there?"

"*Seacat* submerged and going in, sir."

The Admiral nodded.

"We're getting some action from the PT-Boats. At the firing position, sir. P1045 reports P1486 out of station heading fast for firing area, sir."

"What the blazes is he doing? Get P1486. Tell him to hold station. And find out the Captain's name."

"Aye-aye, sir."

"No radio contact with *Playboy* yet, I suppose?"

"We're still trying, Admiral. Nothing yet, sir."

"P1486 reports something on the surface near firing area. Investigating at his own discretion."

"Something like what?"

Pause.

"He says, something like a man in the water, sir."

"OK. Tell him to go in."

"Go IN . . . go in . . . go in . . . closer." Voices.

Hands were lifting him upwards. More pain as his right shoulder bumped against something hard. More voices.

"OK . . . Steady with him . . . He's stopped a bullet . . . Gently now . . . lie him on the catwalk."

Boysie felt himself being stretched out on warm metal. Then a voice he seemed to know.

"Turn away . . . Out of here as fast as you can . . . Full ahead . . . Come . . . Fast."

The throbbing of engines and then a bumping sway. Boysie opened his eyes. Two men in sailor suits were trying to lift him. He saw a portion of catwalk and the scudding sea. Foam bubbling white from sharp bows. Then a hatchway. He was being lowered into a sitting position—into a chair. Consciousness came back with a quick flood. He shook his head—his body being buffeted against the chair. He was in the small, light forward cabin of a fast motor vessel skipping over the sea at speed. And, greatest joy, he was alive. He grinned, prepared to thank his rescuers.

"What happened to the gallant Commander?" asked Gorilka dressed in the uniform of a Lieutenant of the United States Navy. Boysie, for the first time in his life, really wanted to die. This was double-jeopardy with a vengeance.

"Are you all right, Solev?" asked Gorilka, sitting in the bucket seat next to Boysie. In front of him the sailor at the wheel turned and gave Boysie a nod. He was a big brute with a scar under the right eye. Boysie looked past Gorilka to another sailor. Or was it Death standing there in his summer rig? The young sailor had a skull-like face.

"A proper little *memento mori*," murmured Boysie as though in a kind of delirium. Then he closed his eyes and feigned unconsciousness. He really could not cope with any more.

They bandaged Boysie's arm ("A nasty flesh wound," said Gorilka). Now Boysie lay back in the bucket seat—a couple of feet from the sliding hatch leading to the starboard side of the PT-boat's narrow catwalk. By continual lapses into fraudulent swooning, he had, so far, kept Gorilka from questioning him.

"They're still trying to call us up on the radio, boss," said a tubby fake sailor sitting with his back to Gorilka, operating the transmitter. "Other PT-Boat's reported we picked someone up."

"That is all right. Keep them happy. Tell them we have taken a survivor on board and that we are bringing him back to base. Say that he has told us *Playboy* is at the bottom of the ocean, badly damaged."

"You're the boss, boss."

"Solev," said Gorilka gently. "Come along, Solev. Did the Commander set the *Omega* switch."

"Uh?" said Boysie making a tired-eyes look. Then faintly. "*Omega* minus thirty minutes."

"Good boy. We shall have reached safety by then. Good. You have done well, Solev; done very well, Vladimir. You got the *Trepholite* away. We will read all about that in the newspapers tonight. There will be mourning in London. There were no hitches in launching were there?"

Boysie lolled his head. "Homer working. OK. Worked OK."

"Good. Pity about the Commander. How did he go?"

"Later," said Boysie, weakly. "Tell you later."

"All right, Vladimir. Nearly over now." Boysie cringed as he felt the podgy hand patting his knee. Then Gorilka started talking softly in Russian. Oh gawd, thought Boysie. Must rest and keep him from finding out that I am not Solev. "Later," he repeated weaker than ever.

Gorilka was back speaking English. "You just stay nice and quiet, Vladimir. We'll soon have you safe. We head towards the harbour and then turn north at the last minute. We have cars waiting the other side of La Jolla. Within an hour we will be on our way to Los Angeles. Ah, the City of the Angels. Think of that, Vladimir, The City of the Angels."

"HAS THAT goddamned PT-Boat not reported yet?" The Admiral was getting hot and tetchy.

"We seem to have lost contact, sir. I can't get anything from P1486."

"Well, call P1045 and ask if he's observed anything."

"Aye-aye, sir."

Mostyn was feeling the strain of inaction, sitting close to the Admiral who also looked as though he would prefer to be out and about. Birdlip just looked sad and was secretly hoping that everyone had forgotten him.

"P1045 reports P1486 has picked up a man from the sea, sir. Says they have just passed him, heading for base at speed. They waved at him."

"Well, ain't that dandy? Did he wave back?"

"Didn't say, sir."

"Radar?"

"Yes, sir, we have them on the scanner. Moving at speed about thirty-five miles out."

"Well, keep trying to raise 1486."

"Message from *Seacat*, sir. *Playboy* in position and steady. No visible signs of damage."

"Just raised P1486, sir. Say they've picked up a survivor from *Playboy* and are bringing him in. Survivor reports *Playboy* badly damaged and gone to the bottom after premature firing of *Trepholite*."

"Does he now?" The Admiral was going through some hand-clenching and unclenching exercises. Then, firmly, "Take over, Stenway, I'm goin' out to see that survivor myself. My helicopter ready?"

"Aye-aye, sir."

"You coming?" The Admiral turned to Mostyn as he got out of his chair.

"If I may, sir."

"Good."

As they were leaving the dais, a small, experimental voice piped over the speaker system. "Admiral, sir? Budge speaking —in charge of Surface Light Craft. Sir, we have not got a P1486 out there."

"So now he tells me!" The Admiral glared at Mostyn as

though it were all his fault. "Come on." And to Stenway who was taking over at the dais. "Guide my helicopter to that damn PT-Boat. And get that flight of Voodoos within striking distance. Out of the sun!"

"Aye-aye, sir," Stenway, all efficient, was full of himself and his sudden, exalted command.

"And don't balls it up, George. Please," said the Admiral.

MOSTYN AND the Admiral did not talk as the big HOK-1 helicopter chopped its way over the sea. To Mostyn's discomfort, and anxiety, the Admiral insisted on having the large sliding doors open, so there was no protection between the occupants and the open air falling away to dazzling sea, 500 feet below.

"How long?" yelled the Admiral to the naval rating sitting up front with the radio transmitter.

" 'Bout five minutes, sir. Green Flight report, in position, sir. In the sun."

Mostyn looked out at the placid water and wondered about Boysie.

BOYSIE WAS getting the crawling fears again. What would they do when they found he was not Solev—as they surely must? Would he be shipped back to Russia with them? Or (more likely) would the wretched Gorilka devise some ghastly torture leading, remorselessly, to Death.

A sailor-suited thug appeared in the hatchway.

"There's a chopper headin' for us from the shore, boss."

Boysie felt Gorilka move nervously. "All right. We have been successful so far. All will be well."

THEY CAME down to about twenty feet above the sea, sweeping alongside the fast-moving PT-Boat. The Admiral exchanged his binoculars for a hand loudhailer. Mostyn took the binoculars as the helicopter drew in close again. He adjusted the glasses and put them to his eyes. The central section of the PT-Boat came into focus. There, lying back, just inside the cabin hatch, his face turned upwards looking like a trapped rabbit, was Boysie Oakes.

"It's my lad, Admiral. They've got my laddie down there. Can we go get him?" He saw, behind the admiral, another naval rating was loading a heavy sub-machine gun.

They went down again, running with the boat, the Admiral leaning forward half out of the doorway, the loudhailer to his mouth.

"P1486, heave to," he shouted. "We will take off the survivor. Heave to. We have a hammock coming down. D'ye hear me?"

GORILKA SWORE—in English.

"Whaddamytado, boss?" The man at the wheel was still letting the craft snarl through the water at full speed.

"Slow down . . . No . . . Do as he says . . . Heave to . . . When they come in close I will give you the word . . . Not until I say . . . Then blast them . . . Blast them and run for it . . . straight for La Jolla."

Boysie groaned. He wondered it he really was delirious. There might be a chance though. It was only a couple of feet to the hatch and the catwalk. Boysie moved his legs under him and hoped.

The PT-Boat's engines ran down to an idling grumble and she was still, swaying on the water. The helicopter had come round again making its approach from the stern; nearly over them now, down very low, the rope rescue hammock slung out of the wide hole in the side of its vulnerable belly.

"She's too low," muttered the scar-faced man at the wheel. "Blow up on top of us if we blast her from here."

"Wait for it," said Gorilka quietly. "Wait for it. Patience."

Boysie had not worked out how many were aboard the PT-Boat, nor what weapons they intended to use. His eyes were fixed on the hatch. The shadow of the HOK-1 lay right over them now—the hammock brushing against the catwalk and the whirlpool of wind from the rotors flecking the sea and blowing into the cabin. Now it was level with the hatch—three feet, at the most, from Boysie. Biting his lip and holding his right arm to protect the wound. Boysie pushed with his feet, twisted and leaped straight through the hatch, sprawling across the hammock. There was a shout from behind him, then a jerk as the helicopter swung away and upwards. Boysie's stomach descended about thirty feet. He was flying, spread-eagled over the hammock, swinging in an arc, almost bumping the top of the cabin. They were rising fast in a terrifying whirl of noise and shouting. Boysie closed his eyes. Something whined past him thudding against the underside of the helicopter.

"They're shooting, for Chrissake . . ." a voice from above.

"Get the hell out of it!" yelled the Admiral.

The chatter of a machine gun from above and the sudden thud of something heavier from the PT-Boat.

The helicopter accelerated, climbing, turning on its axis and moving away to the stern, its rotor blades whipping through the air, the Pratt and Whitney going wild. The firing was spasmodic, unconcentrated, lacking in confidence. Boysie's leap had taken them by surprise and the helicopter had been badly angled for any real attempt from the PT-Boat. The hammock-winch whirred, and Boysie arrived in the HOK's doorway like a load of freshly netted herrings. They were out of range now, high and turning south in a steady curve.

"Call in those jets. The real thing. My responsibility." The Admiral was hopping mad. "I'll teach 'em to shoot at Charles P. Fullenhaft."

"And at James G. Mostyn," murmured Mostyn.

The radio man was talking quickly into his microphone.

The PT-Boat was still trying to put up a show, firing in earnest from the heavy anti-aircraft cannon for'ard. But the shells were dropping short, spent long before they could reach the HOK-1.

They disentangled Boysie from the hammock. He was the colour of a nicely-ripe Camembert, and the wound was bleeding again.

"What cheer, Boysie old Boysie?" said Mostyn. "You are Boysie, aren't you?"

Boysie could not help himself. He tried hard, but nature took over and he was violently sick, right over Mostyn's brown aniline calf shoes.

"Yes," said Mostyn, gingerly shaking one foot after the other. "yes. It's our Boysie. The Boysie we know and love. The uncrushable flip-top spy."

"Look at 'em go," called the Admiral. Out of the sun two of the Voodoo jets were screaming in towards the PT-Boat. The Admiral turned to Mostyn, "That's what they mean when they talk about calling down the wrath of the Almighty," he said.

THE FLIGHT Leader brought his Voodoo down to fifty feet. His wingman was to his left—slightly behind him in case they needed a second strike.

"This baby's all mine," said the Flight Leader to himself as the rocket sights came on to the PT-Boat—a toy on a blue lake. He could see men diving over the side, panicking with fear exploding among them like a sticky bomb. There was a small fat man in naval uniform standing in the cabin hatchway waving a stick. He looked as though he was shouting.

The Flight Leader pressed the rocket release, cased back on the control column and took his jet up in a tight climbing turn. He levelled out and banked steeply, looking down the wing to see if the strike had gone home.

Both rockets hit—converging just aft of the cabin. Across the quiet water a hand-shaped crest of flame splayed out, then died. The PT-Boat keeled over, fire and smoke spurting from her broken innards. The pilot could see another PT-Boat coming up fast on the Admiral's orders; and away to the east, the Old Man's helicopter, like a grotesque insect, chattering back towards San Diego Harbour, peaceful in the afternoon sunshine.

EPILOGUE: DOUBLE DATE
San Diego, July

"BOYSIE DARLING, you've been wonderful." Priscilla Braddock-Fairchild gave a little moue of pleasure, leaned across the table at the exotic *Bali Hai*, and grasped Boysie's free hand. Even after three weeks—with the wound almost healed—Boysie granted himself the luxury of wearing a glamorous sling.

They had only kept him in hospital for a week. There had been a personal letter of thanks from the Prime Minister and an invitation to dine at Number 10—date unspecified. Since then it had been fun almost all the way. The fears were gone. The terrors had flown (except, perhaps, for the nagging worry about flying back to London with Mostyn tomorrow).

Four of the PT-Boat's crew had been picked up alive—including a twenty-year-old boy with a face like a skull. Of Gorilka there had been no trace. *Playboy* had been brought to the surface by the early evening of that dramatic day when *Operation Understrike* failed. Surprisingly, Gorilka had really only given Braddock-Fairchild pellets containing a mild nerve gas. The six observers, the Radar Officer and the rest of the crew were found unconscious but alive, oblivious to what had occurred. There had been a funeral, with full naval honours, for those killed on the Control Deck of *Playboy*. Commander Braddock-Fairchild, RN, was quietly cremated. Apart from his daughter, there had been only two mourners—Boysie Oakes and James George Mostyn.

The remainder of Boysie's time in San Diego was spent keeping a lot of distance between Chicory and Priscilla (who had not taken her treacherous father's death much to heart). Boysie had run riot with ruses and cunning wiles. Tales of conferences with the Admiral, or dinner with his boss, Mostyn, managed to keep both the girls, and Boysie happy. But he had to admit that after a fortnight he was getting hard pressed, and running out of excuses.

At this moment he was dining with Priscilla. As far as Chicory was concerned, he was having a farewell drink with the officers at North Island Naval Base. Priscilla was making the most of the evening, for she knew he had promised to have drinks with the officers at the North Island Naval Base when he left her at midnight (when Chicory was expecting him in her suite at the *El Cortez*). Life was becoming very complicated.

The dinner had been right for the evening—which was sultry with the moon riding high over the Bay, and an off-shore breeze tickling the palm tops, and all that travel bureau goo. Jar Won Ton (Chinese raviolo) was followed by a speciality of the house—Chicken of the Gods: breast of chicken sauted in Chinese wine and spices, rolled in Waterchestnut flour, deep-fried and served with white sauce and Sesame pods. They had finished with fresh Hawaian Pineapple, and Boysie was just wondering if they would have time before he had to meet Chicory. But Priscilla had stopped holding his hand and leaning over the table. She was not even looking at him any more, but at a point to the left of his shoulder. He sensed someone near him.

"So this is North Island Base and these are the nice officers you're having drinks with, hu?" Chicory was standing by the table, her cheeks flushed in the traditional manner of a woman on whom infidelity had been practised.

Priscilla quickly recovered her poise.

"Who is this person, Boysie?" she asked.

"Ahrrghurr . . ." began Boysie, when a smooth voice mercifully intruded from the other side of the table.

"Hallo Boysie," said Mostyn, a gleaming blonde on his arm. "Cable arrived for you. Thought it might be urgent, so Tibby and I brought it down. From England?"

"Ah . . . I . . . expect . . . so," said Boysie precisely. He knew darned well the cable was from England. He had cabled Elizabeth yesterday morning during a brief moment of nostalgia.

This would be her reply. Mostyn might not be such a blessing after all.

"Why don't you open it then, old Boysie?"

"Yea, open it," said Chicory, leaning over the table.

Priscilla got up, came over and stood behind him, a hand on his shoulder.

"Open it, Boysie darling."

He felt Chicory's hand on his other shoulder.

"Should if I were you, old boy," said Mostyn. "They'll probably tear you apart if you don't."

Probably tear me apart if I do, thought Boysie. Resigned he ripped open the envelope with his teeth (not having a spare hand) and spread out the paper for all to see.

SO HAPPY TO GET YOUR CABLE STOP WILL MEET YOU WITH CAR AT LONDON AIRPORT STOP FORTNIGHT IN PARIS WITH YOU A WONDERFUL IDEA STOP MISSING YOU TERRIBLY STOP ALL AND DEEPEST LOVE STOP ELIZABETH

"And who's Elizabeth?" chorused Chicory and Priscilla in unison, their grips tightening.

"Ah . . . Yes . . . Now I'm glad you asked me that," said Boysie.

Wyndham Books are obtainable from many booksellers and newsagents. If you have any difficulty please send purchase price plus postage on the scale below to:

Wyndham Cash Sales,
P.O. Box 11,
Falmouth,
Cornwall

OR

Star Book Service,
G.P.O. Box 29,
Douglas,
Isle of Man,
British Isles

While every effort is made to keep prices low, it is sometimes necessary to increase prices at short notice. Wyndham Books reserve the right to show new retail prices on covers which may differ from those advertised in the text or elsewhere.

Postage and Packing Rate
U.K.
One book 25p plus 10p per copy for each additional book ordered to a maximum charge of £1.05

B.F.P.O. and Eire
One book 25p plus 10p per copy for the next 8 books and thereafter 5p per book. Overseas 40p for the first book and 12p per copy for each additional book.